He wanted to argue with her, the urge to spill the whole ugly tale so powerful it felt like poison in his gut.

His leg was bad. It couldn't do the same things he'd once asked of it. But he was stronger now than he had been in the middle of that burning hell.

He'd never known that level of utter helplessness before in his life. He prayed to God he'd never know it again.

He willed Susannah to step back from him, to take away her soft warmth, her sweet scent, her gentle, disarming gaze.

Of course, being Susannah, she stepped closer, her hands lifting to his cheeks, ensnaring him. "I have no idea what to say to you," she said, her voice a whisper. "I don't know what you need."

You, he thought with growing dismay. *I just need you.*

BONEYARD RIDGE

—

PAULA GRAVES

HARLEQUIN® INTRIGUE®

For all the wounded warriors who put their lives and their
bodies on the line every day to make the world a safer place.
God bless you, and thank you for all you do.

ISBN-13: 978-0-373-74850-1

Recycling programs
for this product may
not exist in your area.

Boneyard Ridge

Copyright © 2014 by Paula Graves

All rights reserved. Except for use in any review, the reproduction or
utilization of this work in whole or in part in any form by any electronic,
mechanical or other means, now known or hereinafter invented, including
xerography, photocopying and recording, or in any information storage
or retrieval system, is forbidden without the written permission of the
publisher, Harlequin Enterprises Limited, 225 Duncan Mill Road,
Don Mills, Ontario M3B 3K9, Canada.

This is a work of fiction. Names, characters, places and incidents are
either the product of the author's imagination or are used fictitiously,
and any resemblance to actual persons, living or dead, business
establishments, events or locales is entirely coincidental.

This edition published by arrangement with Harlequin Books S.A.

For questions and comments about the quality of this book,
please contact us at CustomerService@Harlequin.com.

® and TM are trademarks of Harlequin Enterprises Limited or its
corporate affiliates. Trademarks indicated with ® are registered in the
United States Patent and Trademark Office, the Canadian Intellectual
Property Office and in other countries.

Printed in U.S.A.

www.Harlequin.com

ABOUT THE AUTHOR

Alabama native Paula Graves wrote her first book, a mystery starring herself and her neighborhood friends, at the age of six. A voracious reader, Paula loves books that pair tantalizing mystery with compelling romance. When she's not reading or writing, she works as a creative director for a Birmingham advertising agency and spends time with her family and friends. She is a member of Southern Magic Romance Writers, Heart of Dixie Romance Writers and Romance Writers of America. Paula invites readers to visit her website, www.paulagraves.com.

Books by Paula Graves

HARLEQUIN INTRIGUE

CAST OF CHARACTERS

Hunter Bragg—The former Army Sergeant may not be in the service anymore, but he still has a life-or-death mission: go undercover to stop a domestic terror group from killing an innocent woman who could interfere with their deadly plot.

Susannah Marsh—The pretty, polished event planner stands in the way of a plan to target a law enforcement conference, and her only chance of surviving is a scruffy hotel maintenance man who is anything but what he seems. But can she trust anyone, especially since she's hiding deadly secrets of her own?

Billy Dawson—The current head of the Blue Ridge Infantry has deadly plans for the upcoming law enforcement conference.

Marcus Lemonde—Susannah's right-hand man has to take over her job when she's forced to run for her life. Will he be next on the target list?

Asa Bradbury—The head of a brutal mountain crime family is out for revenge, and he's finally got a lead on his brother's killer.

Alexander Quinn—The former CIA agent has put a lot of faith in Hunter Bragg to handle the dangerous undercover assignment. But does he have another agenda where Hunter is concerned?

Prologue

Smoky Joe's Saloon had never pretended to be anything more than a hillbilly honky-tonk, a hole in the wall on Old Purgatory Road that served cold beer, peanuts roasted in the shell and a prodigious selection of Merle Haggard hits on the ancient jukebox in the corner.

At the moment, "The Fightin' Side of Me" blasted through the jukebox's tinny speakers, an apt sound track for the bar brawl brewing around the pool table in the corner.

Two men circled the table like a pair of wary Pit Bulls, eyes locked in silent combat. The older of the two was also the drunker, a heavyset man with bloodshot eyes and a misshapen nose, mottled by red spider veins. He seemed to be the aggressor, from Alexander Quinn's vantage point at a table in the corner of the small bar, but the younger, leaner man had shown no signs of trying to de-escalate the tension.

On the contrary, an almost frantic light

gleamed in his green eyes, a feral hunger for conflict that Quinn had noticed the first time he'd ever laid eyes on the man.

His name was Hunter Bragg, and he'd finally found the trouble he'd been looking for all night.

"Come on, Toby, you know he's going to beat the hell out of you the second you take a swing. Then I'm going to have to call the police and you've already got a couple of D and Ds on your record this year, don't you?" The reasonable question, uttered in a tone that wavered somewhere between sympathy and annoyance, came from the bartender, a burly man in his early sixties with shoulder-length salt-and-pepper hair and a gray-streaked beard. He was dressed like most of the patrons, in jeans and a camouflage jacket over a T-shirt that had been through the wash a few times, dulling its original navy color to a smoky slate blue.

He was the "Joe" of Smoky Joe's Saloon, Joe Breslin, an Army vet who'd opened the bar with his savings after deciding not to re-up decades earlier when the trouble in Panama was starting to heat up. He'd packed on a few pounds and lost a few steps since his military days, but Quinn had seen him in action a few nights earlier when another loudmouthed drunk had taken the angry young man's bait and lived to regret it.

"He's askin' for an ass-kickin', Joe!" the man

named Toby complained, shooting a baleful look at Hunter Bragg. "I don't care if he *is* a damn war hero."

"I'm no hero," Bragg growled, the feral grin never faltering.

"Bragg, I don't want to kick you out of my bar, I really don't," Joe said. "But if you don't shut your damn trap and stop picking fights, I'm gonna. You think your sister needs any more trouble?"

Bragg's gaze snapped toward the bartender at the mention of his sister. "Shut up."

Breslin held up his hands. "Just sayin'. She's already got enough on her plate, don't she?"

"Shut up!" Bragg howled, the sound of a wounded animal. Chill bumps scattered down Alexander Quinn's spine and, on instinct, his hand went to the pistol hidden under his jacket.

Toby took a couple of staggering steps backward until he bumped into the wall, dislodging some darts from the board that hung near the pool table. "You're crazy, man."

Bragg's head snapped back toward Toby, barely leashed violence throbbing in his tight muscles. Quinn wasn't sure if the man had come to the bar armed or not; Joe Breslin wasn't the sort of proprietor who made people check their weapons at the door. And so far, Bragg had never used anything but his fists in a fight.

But things could turn disastrous in a heartbeat, Quinn knew. He'd seen it happen too many times.

He crossed the room with quiet speed, inserting himself into the arena of conflict. As he'd hoped, his mere presence put a big dent in the tension, as both men turned their wary gazes toward him.

"Gentlemen," he said with a polite nod. "Are you still using this table?"

Toby stared at him as if he were crazy, but Bragg's eyes narrowed, his head tilting a notch to one side.

"I know you," he said.

Quinn nodded. "We've met."

"In Afghanistan?"

Quinn shook his head. "At Landstuhl."

Bragg's face blanched visibly at the mention of the military hospital in Germany where combat-injured American troops were treated until they were stable enough to return to the States for further treatment.

Bragg had spent over a week there after an improvised explosive device, or IED, had obliterated his troop transport vehicle, killing everyone else in the Humvee and leaving Bragg with a mangled leg and a head injury. Surgeons had saved the leg, though when Quinn had seen the man in the hospital in Germany, there had been some question as to whether he'd have much use of the limb again.

Now, it seemed, it was the head injury that should have caused the doctors more concern. Bragg's limp was barely noticeable these days. But he was no longer the good-natured practical joker his fellow soldiers had nicknamed the Tennessee Tornado.

"You brass?" Bragg asked warily.

"Civilian," Quinn answered.

The green eyes narrowed further, little more than slits in his stormy face. "Spook?"

Quinn just smiled.

Bragg's eyebrows rose slightly, opening his eyes enough that Quinn could read the sudden recognition in the younger man's gaze. "You're the guy who runs that new PI joint over in Purgatory."

Quinn removed his hand from his jacket pocket, producing a simple, cream-colored business card. "The Gates," he said, holding out the card.

Hesitantly, Bragg took the card from Quinn's outstretched hand. "I'm not in the market for a private eye."

"I'm in the market for employees."

Bragg handed the card back. "I've got a job."

"You sweep floors at the Piggly Wiggly."

"It's honest work."

"So's this." Quinn held up the card.

"I'm not looking for excitement."

Quinn merely lifted one eyebrow, shooting a look toward Toby, who stood next to the dartboard, watching Quinn and Bragg with a confused expression on his whiskey-slackened face.

Putting the card on the green felt surface of the pool table, Quinn looked back at Bragg. "If you change your mind."

He left the bar without looking back to see if Bragg picked up the card. He couldn't make the decision for the man. He could only offer an option that might channel his anger in a more productive direction.

He wasn't in the business of saving people from themselves, no matter what the good folks of Purgatory seemed to think.

Chapter One

"Damn it!" Susannah Marsh looked with dismay at the jagged chip in her French-manicured thumbnail and mentally calculated whether or not she could work in a trip to the salon over the next seventy-two hours.

Nope. Not a hope in hell.

"What's the matter?" Marcus Lemonde looked up from his desk in the corner of the small office, the expression on his narrow face suggesting the query was more about politeness than interest.

"Broke a nail, and I won't have time between now and the conference to get it fixed."

"Can't you just file it down or something?" Even his feigned attempt at interest disappeared, swallowed by mild annoyance.

She sighed, knowing she'd be just as annoyed in his position. It hadn't been that long ago she'd have rolled her eyes at a manicure mishap herself. "Yeah. I'll do that." Because a perfect French manicure was so easy to achieve, especially when one nail was now considerably shorter than the rest.

How on earth had she managed to choose a career where things like manicures and stiletto-heeled shoes practically came with the job description? Lord, if the kids she used to run around with back on Boneyard Ridge could see her now...

She dug through her purse for the manicure kit she always kept with her, but it wasn't there. Had she left it in another purse? No, she distinctly remembered getting it out of yesterday's bag that morning.

And leaving it on the breakfast bar in her apartment.

Damn it, damn it, *damn it!*

The resort had a gift shop at the far end of the hotel that carried things like nail files and other items hotel guests might have forgotten to pack. But she barely had time to get to her meeting with the Tri-State Law Enforcement Society's representatives, who were meeting with her and hotel security to go over last-minute plans for the conference that would start on Friday.

With a glance at Marcus to make sure he wasn't watching, she dipped her hand into her purse and grabbed the slightly bulky Swiss Army knife she also kept with her at all times. Its attached file was a bit rough for a good manicure, but it would do for the meeting. Then she could run down to the gift shop for a nail kit to do the job right.

Flipping open the nail file as she hurried down the corridor, she bit back a laugh. All this drama for a broken nail!

For the first sixteen years of her life, she'd chewed her nails to stubs and never thought twice about it. She'd owned one purse at a time, which she carried only when absolutely necessary. Skirts were the bane of her existence, baring as they did the scars of a lifetime of scratches and scrapes, and high heels were so far off her radar she'd had to spend a whole week of secret practice sessions with her cousin from Raleigh before she could navigate her way across the room in a pair.

How had she turned into such a girl?

The obvious answer was leaving Boneyard Ridge, making a new life for herself in a world where little redneck tomboys from the hills could easily find themselves chewed up and spit out before they could blink twice.

She wasn't going to let her grandmother down, the way everyone else always figured she'd do.

As she waited for the elevator to the third floor, where Ken Dailey, head of Highland Hotel and Resort's security team, would be waiting for her with three of the law-enforcement society's event organizers, she ran the coarse file across her nail, wincing as it snagged heavily on the broken edge. The friction, she saw with dismay, was doing horrible things to the French tip polish. Giving up on the nail-file attachment, she flipped open the scissors and snipped off the whole tip of the broken nail.

The elevator dinged and the doors swept smoothly open just as she snapped the scissors back into the knife handle. She quickly dropped the knife into the pocket of her jacket and pasted on a smile to greet whoever might be inside the elevator car.

There was only one other occupant, a scruffy-looking man wearing a maintenance-crew jumpsuit. His green eyes lifted in surprise as he pulled up to keep from running straight into her.

"Sorry," he said in a voice as deep as a mountain cavern. He stepped back into the elevator to let her in.

"You aren't getting out?" she asked.

"I pushed the button for the wrong floor." His gaze dropping, he reached out and started to push the button for the third floor, then looked sheepish when he realized it was already lit up.

He was a rangy man in his early thirties, with shaggy dark hair that fell into his darting eyes, making him appear to be looking at her from under a hood. He would probably be nice-look-

ing if he didn't come across as such a sad sack,
Susannah thought, torn between pity for his obvious discomfort and irritation that he wouldn't
lift his head and look her in the eye.

He had spoken in a strong hill-country twang,
reminiscent of the harsh mountain accent she'd
ruthlessly subdued since leaving Boneyard Ridge.

"Grubby little tomboys from here don't get to
live out their dreams, Susie," her grandmother
had told her as she handed Susannah $400 in
cash and a bus ticket to Raleigh. "You gotta learn
how to make it out there in the real world."

The maintenance man let her off the elevator
first when they reached the third floor. She moved
ahead, trying to ignore the prickle on the back of
her neck as he brought up the rear. He didn't over-
take her, despite his longer legs. When she stopped
to straighten her clothes before entering Meeting
Room C, she spared a quick glance his way.

He kept his head down, apparently determined
not to meet her gaze as he passed behind her. He
walked with a strangely deliberate gait, as if each
step were a decision he had to make before he
committed himself to the next one. A couple of
steps later, she figured out why. He had a limp.

She couldn't remember ever seeing him around
the hotel before, but maintenance workers and
hospitality staffers had a pretty high turnover
rate. Plus, while she wasn't someone who saw

the people who pushed mops and brooms as interchangeable drones, the stress and speed of her job as the resort's head events coordinator meant she didn't have the time or opportunity to get to know many people outside of her own office.

For that matter, she thought as she pasted on her best go-getter smile and opened the door to the meeting room, she barely knew the staff in her own office, including Marcus, her right-hand man. They rarely had time for chitchat and she wasn't one to socialize with her coworkers off the clock. Or anyone else, for that matter.

She couldn't afford friends.

Four men awaited her in the meeting room, Ken Dailey with hotel security and three others. They stood in a cluster near the large picture window that offered a spectacular view of the mist-shrouded Smoky Mountains to the east.

She looked with envy at their cups of coffee but knew she didn't have time to get a cup of her own. They had business to discuss, and she was running out of daylight.

"Gentlemen, sorry I'm late," she said, even though she knew full well she was at least five minutes early to the meeting. "We have a lot to cover, so shall we get to work?"

HUNTER BRAGG STOPPED at the end of the hallway and turned back toward the meeting rooms clustered in the center of this wing of the hotel. The door closed shut behind her, and he started to relax, shoving his hair out of his face and straightening his back.

She hadn't recognized him from the news reports. He hadn't really feared she would, given how different he looked from the clean-cut Army sergeant whose abduction had been a weeklong sensation until something new came along to take over the news cycle.

Of course, he'd recognized her easily from the photo Billy Dawson had shown him and the men he'd selected for the job a few days earlier. "Her name is Susannah Marsh. She's in our way. Y'all are gonna take her out."

In that photograph, taken by a telephoto lens from the woods that hemmed in the resort's employee parking lot, Susannah Marsh had given off a definite aura of money and sophistication. Her well-tailored suit, the shimmery green of a mallard's head, and shiny black high heels had offered an intoxicating blend of power and sexuality that had sent the other militia members privy to the plan into flights of lustful fancy.

All Hunter had been able to think about was the fact that Billy and the others—men he'd spent the last three months befriending—wanted him to take part in killing a woman just because she was in the way of their plans.

They seemed so ordinary on the outside. Billy Dawson fixed cars out of his garage for a living. Morris Bell drove a Ridge County school bus. Delbert Yarnell worked at the hardware store in Barrowville. They had wives and kids.

And a festering hatred of authority.

Down the hall, the elevator dinged and the doors swished open. A well-dressed man in a silk suit and shiny wingtips stepped out and started to turn away from the end of the hall where Hunter stood, but his gaze snapped back in his direction and he changed course, his long strides eating up the distance between them.

"What are you doing up here?" he asked, frowning.

The question caught Hunter by surprise. He didn't know this man, though he looked vaguely familiar. They'd probably passed each other in the halls at some point in the last week.

But why was this man challenging him?

The other man's nostrils flared. "You can't afford to make her suspicious of you."

Hunter blinked. This man was part of Dawson's crew, too?

"Don't worry," he assured the other man aloud. "She sees me as part of the wallpaper."

"We're making our move tonight."

Hunter's gut clenched. Tonight? Nothing was supposed to go down until tomorrow. What had happened? And why hadn't Billy Dawson warned him of the change in plans?

"I know," he bluffed. "What's the plan?"

The other man narrowed his eyes. "Billy didn't tell me to share it with you."

"I thought we were on the same side."

"Are we?"

Hunter returned the other man's skeptical gaze with a cold, hard stare of his own. "Think I'd be cleaning toilets in this place if we weren't?"

The other man straightened his tie, a nervous habit, obviously, since his tie was already immaculately straight. "Just don't screw this up."

"Wouldn't dream of it."

Without another word, the man in the suit turned and strode away from Hunter as quickly as he'd approached.

Releasing tension in a quiet sigh, Hunter turned the corner and headed for the stairs. Once he was safely out of sight, he pulled his phone from his pocket and hit "one" on his speed dial.

When the voice on the other end answered, he said, "They're moving up the hit."

"To when?"

"Tonight, as soon as she leaves the office." Muscles in Hunter's gut quivered as he tried not to panic. "It's too soon."

There was a brief moment of thick silence

before the other man asked, "Any idea when she'll leave the office?"

"Going by her usual schedule, no earlier than six. Probably closer to seven."

"Any idea what they're planning to do?"

"No. I didn't quite make it into the inner circle before this all went down. I've been trying to piece things together, but—" He bit back a frustrated sigh. "I don't know what they're planning. Or where."

"I can try to get some backup into place for you by tonight, but I'm not sure I can swing it before then. I'll see how many people I can move into place by tonight, but you know we're stretched pretty thin at the moment, until I can bring in more new hires."

"I know," Hunter answered tersely. He knew exactly how understaffed The Gates was, if Quinn had resorted to hiring an ex-soldier with a bum leg and anger-management issues.

"You may have to handle this alone for a little while." Another brief pause, then, "Can you?"

"I guess I'll have to, won't I?" Hunter answered, unable to conceal a touch of bitterness in his voice.

SHE NEEDED A PET, Susannah decided as she crossed the darkened employee parking lot. A pet would give her an excuse to leave the office at a reasonable hour instead of finding just one more thing to take care of before she locked the door for the day.

Not a dog. Dogs needed room to run and someone home to let them out for potty breaks. A cat, maybe. Cats were independent. She'd always liked cats. She'd cried for weeks when she'd had to leave her marmalade tabby Poco behind when she left Boneyard Ridge.

She'd left a lot of things behind in Boneyard Ridge. Things she'd never get back again.

She'd parked at the far end of the parking lot when she'd arrived at work that morning, on the premise that the long walk across the blacktop to her office would be almost as good as working out.

Almost. Pulling out her phone, she hit the record button. "Look into joining a gym."

"You don't look like you need one."

The masculine drawl came out of the darkness, sending her bones rattling with surprise. The lamp at this end of the parking lot was out, she realized as she turned in a circle, trying to spot the speaker.

A darker shadow loomed out of the gloom surrounding her car. She instantly regretted not shelling out a few more bucks to get an alarm system with a remote. She peered toward the approaching figure, taking a couple of defensive steps backward.

"I'm not going to hurt you," the man's voice assured her.

She didn't believe him.

Sliding her hand into the pocket of her purse, she closed her fingers around the small canister of pepper spray she made a point of carrying.

"Don't do that," the man warned, a hint of steel in his deep voice. "We don't have time."

Even as the words rumbled from the gathering gloom, Susannah heard the growl of a car engine starting nearby. She saw the shadowy figure shift attention toward the sound, and she took the opening, kicking off her high heels and running toward the lights of the hotel behind her.

She didn't get three steps before he grabbed her from behind, wrapping her upper body in a firm grip and lifting her off her feet so quickly she didn't even have time to scream before his hand clapped over her mouth.

She tried to pull the pepper spray from her purse, but his hold on her was unshakable. She could barely flex her fingers.

The roar of the engine grew closer, and she started kicking backward against her captor's legs. Her only reward was pain in her own heels as they slammed against what felt like solid rock.

"For God's sake, stop fighting me!" He was

running with her, ignoring her attempts to get away as he loped across the parking lot toward the woods beyond. "I'm on your side."

The sheer audacity of his growling assurance spurred her fury, and she clamped down on his hand with her teeth.

A stream of curses rewarded her effort, but the man didn't let her go. He just kept running, an oddly hitching stride that tugged at her memory until she realized where she'd heard that low, cavernous voice before.

The sad-sack maintenance man.

It's always the quiet ones....

Suddenly, a loud stuttering sound seemed to fill the air around them, and her captor shoved her to the ground and threw himself over her body, pinning her in place. Her purse went flying, pepper spray and all.

The least of her worries, she realized as her rattled mind finally identified the sound. Gunfire. Her pulse started whooshing like thunder in her ears as she held her breath for the sound of more shots.

The engine noise she'd heard before faded, followed by the unmistakable squeal of tire on pavement. They were turning around and coming back for another go, she realized, her breath freezing in her lungs.

The man on top of her pushed himself off

her, giving her a brief chance to flee his grasp. But she was too paralyzed with shock to make a move, and then the moment had passed. He grabbed her arm, dragging her to her feet, and started running.

As she stumbled behind him, she realized she had only two stark options—run with him or put up a fight that would give whoever had just tried to gun her down another chance to finish the job.

Her heart hammering wildly in her chest, she ran.

Chapter Two

Night had leached all the warmth from the hills, leaving behind a bitter, damp cold that bit all the way to the marrow. The collection of bone fragments, steel plates and screws holding his left leg together joined forces in a cacophony of pain, but Hunter ignored the aches and kept moving.

He wasn't sure what the men with the guns would do once they realized he'd spirited their target away, but he knew whatever punishment they chose would be brutal and deadly.

Not getting caught was the only option.

A hiss of pain escaped Susannah's lips, but he couldn't let her stop running. Not yet. He could hear the sound of pursuers crashing through the woods behind them, a stark reminder of the consequences of being captured.

"Please," she groaned, tugging at his hand until he slowed the pace, sparing a second to look at her.

In the faint moon glow slanting through the

canopy of trees overhead, Susannah's dark eyes
gazed up at him in pain and fear. "My feet," she
whispered.

He looked down and saw she was barefoot.
Blood stained her toes, and he thought about the
hard, rocky trail they'd just crossed.

Damn it.

Scanning the woods around them, he spotted
a rocky outcropping due east. "Get on my back,"
he said.

She stared back at him, her mouth trembling
open. "What?"

"You either run on those feet or you get on my
back. Or you stay here and let those guys back
there catch up with you."

Her jaw squared. "Who are they? Who are
you?"

He tried not to lose his patience, even though
the sound of the chasers behind them seemed
closer than ever. "They're the people shooting at
you. I'm the guy who's offering to be your damn
mule if you'll just shut up and get on my back."

Her mouth flattened to a thin line of anger, but
she limped toward him as he bent at the knees,
grimacing at the strain on his bad leg, and let
her climb onto his back. He grabbed her thighs
to hold her in place, surprised and annoyed at
how the feel of her firm flesh beneath his fingers

sent a sharp, undeniable arrow of lust straight to his groin,

Not the time, Bragg. Really not the time.

She wasn't a featherweight, but running with a heavy load on his back wasn't exactly a new thing to Hunter after two tours of duty in the Army. He'd been looking for a test of his reconstructed leg, hadn't he? Here it was.

It was lucky the rock outcropping was only a half mile distant, he reflected once they reached it and he put her down to rest for a few seconds while he searched the granite wall for any sign of a nook or alcove in the rock face. He found it seconds before he decided to give up and started back toward where he'd left Susannah, only to find that she was a few feet behind, her eyes wide and haunted.

"What are we doing?" she asked in a hushed tone.

"Hiding," he answered succinctly, sweeping her up into his arms.

She made a soft hiss of surprise but didn't resist as he carried her through the dark opening into a cold, black abyss.

No LIGHT. No sound but that of air flowing in and out of their lungs, fast and harsh in the deep, endless void. After a few seconds, even that sound settled into the faintest of whispers, easily eclipsed by the roar of Susannah's pulse in her ears.

A sliver of deep gray relieved the darkness after a few moments, as her eyes adjusted. The narrow mouth of the cavern, she realized. The only way out. Or in.

If she weren't so bloody terrified, she might find a spot of bleak humor in the idea of being curled up in the hard-muscled arms of a man she knew only as "the sad-sack maintenance man," her bare feet bruised and bleeding, while they hid in a cave from unidentified gunmen.

It was like one of those movies her grandmother liked to watch on cable, the ones where the women were all beautiful, noble victims who inexplicably spent years being treated like garbage by the men in their lives before they finally found their backbones and fought back.

To hell with being a victim, she thought. "What's your name?" she whispered. Because he clearly wasn't the sad sack she'd thought. And if he was just a maintenance man, she was the Queen of England.

"Hunter," he answered after a moment.

"Susannah," she whispered back. "I guess you know that already, though."

"Yeah." His grip on her tightened convulsively, as if he was about to drop her. She grabbed his shoulders in reaction, her fingers digging into an impressive set of muscles.

"Sorry," he whispered.

"You can put me down."

He eased her down until she stood upright, her sore feet flattening on the cold rock floor of the cave. "What happened to your shoes?"

"I kicked them off to run from you. I thought I'd be crossing nice flat concrete, not rocky soil."

"Sorry," he repeated.

He sounded as if he really was sorry, she realized. Of course, maybe that's what he wanted her to think. Maybe he was trying to lull her into being a docile captive.

But two could play that game. If he thought she had decided to go along agreeably, he might drop his guard sooner, giving her a chance to make a break for it.

"You really don't know who those people out there are?" she asked, not believing it for a second.

He didn't answer. Now that she was on her feet, he'd moved slightly away, although she could still feel the furnacelike heat of his body close by, helping cut the biting cold of the cave.

A few seconds later, when it became clear he had no intention of answering her previous question, she asked, "How long before they give up?"

"They don't," he replied.

She'd been afraid of that: "Then how do we get out of here?"

He didn't answer right away, and she felt more than saw him move toward the cave entrance.

She followed, noting with some dismay that while the pain in her feet had lessened, it was mainly because the cold had begun to render them numb. He edged over, giving her an opening to look outside with him, and she slid into the narrow space, her arm brushing his. He really was very muscular, she thought as she peered into the misty gloom.

Scudding clouds gathered overhead, blotting out most of the moonlight filtering through the trees. The darkness outside loomed like a physical entity, threatening and impenetrable.

"Rain's comin'," Hunter whispered, his drawl pronounced. Definitely a mountain native, she thought.

"Is that good or bad?" she asked.

He gave a little shrug, his shoulder sliding against hers. Heat slithered down her arm into her fingertips, catching her off guard.

Good God, woman, she scolded herself silently, inching her arm away from his. *He's your captor. And not in a good way.*

"I don't see anyone out there," he whispered after a few minutes. "I think if we go a little deeper into this cave, we might risk a light."

"A light?"

"Flashlight," he said softly, tugging her with him away from the cave entrance. She stepped gingerly after him, less from pain than from the fear that her numb feet wouldn't know it even if she were walking across a field of broken glass.

A few seconds later, a beam of light slanted across the damp cave walls, illuminating the tight space they occupied. The cave was narrow but surprisingly long, twisting out of sight into the rock wall. Hunter swept the light across the visible space, as if reassuring himself they were alone.

"No bears?" she whispered, quelling a shudder.

"Not at the moment." He flashed an unexpected smile, baring straight white teeth and a surprising pair of dimples high on each cheek. A flutter of raw female awareness vibrated low in her belly, and she jerked her gaze away, appalled by her reaction.

His hand brushed lightly down one arm, scattering goose bumps where he touched her. He closed his fingers around her wrist, his grip solid but gentle. "Let's take a quick look at your feet." He tugged her with him toward a shelflike slab of rock jutting out from the cave wall. "Sit."

She complied, wincing as the coldness of the rock blasted right through her skirt and underwear to chill her backside.

"Sorry. Didn't bring a seat warmer."

But he had brought supplies, she saw with growing alarm, as he reached into the pocket of his jacket and withdrew a soft-sided zippered bag that contained a compact stash of first-aid supplies.

Had he known beforehand that he was going to need to treat a wound?

He ripped open a packet and the sharp tang of rubbing alcohol cut through the musty odor of the cave. "This is gonna sting," he warned a split second before he wiped the alcohol swab across one of the jagged scrapes on the bottom of her foot.

"Son of a—" She clamped her teeth shut and gripped the edge of the outcropping doubling as her seat.

"Sorry." Once again, he sounded sincere, making her feel off balance.

He worked quickly, efficiently, as if he was used to offering aid. Hell, maybe he was. Maybe he was some sort of psychotic cross between Dr. McDreamy and Hannibal Lecter. Emphasis on the McDreamy, she added silently as she watched the muscles of his back flex visibly beneath the thick leather jacket he wore.

He couldn't conjure up a new pair of shoes from his little first-aid kit, but he did wrap her feet in a liberal amount of gauze. As footwear, the gauze didn't have a chance of lasting through another wild hike through the woods, but for the moment, the gauze was bringing her numb feet back to tingling, aching life.

She was beginning to wish they were still numb.

With her feet safely bandaged, Hunter turned off the flashlight, plunging them back into icy blackness. The shocking change from light to dark sent another hard shiver through Susannah's chilled body.

Then warmth washed over her as Hunter settled on the rocky seat next to her, his hip pressed firmly against hers. She felt his arm wrap around her shoulder, and even though she wanted to pull away from his touch, the sheer relief his vibrant heat offered her shivering body was too much of a comfort to rebuff.

With a silent promise to grow a backbone as soon as she could feel her fingers and toes again, she nestled closer to his heat.

HE'D LOST HIS cell phone. In the greater scheme of his present troubles, it wasn't the worst thing that could have happened to him out there in the woods, but it was bad. How was he supposed to call in the cavalry—assuming Quinn could assemble one—if he didn't have his phone?

Beside him, Susannah Marsh had finally stopped shivering, her soft curves molding themselves to the hard planes of his own body. He'd felt her tighten up when he'd first slipped his arm around her, but she was a sensible woman. Even if she thought he was a crazy kidnapper—and really, she'd be an idiot not to—she surely saw the wisdom of letting him keep her from sinking into hypothermia.

"I'm not a crazy kidnapper," he whispered, feeling foolish but unable to stop the words from slipping between his lips.

She stiffened beside him. "What proof can you offer in your defense?"

"I wasn't the one with the guns?" Well, technically he did have a gun, a subcompact Glock 26 tucked in an ankle holster. But if he told her that—

"No, you're the one who accosted me in the parking lot, dragged me barefoot through the woods and told me I had to run or die."

"Those were the only choices at the moment."

She sat up, away from his grasp, and cold air slithered into the space between them. Only a whisper of ambient light seeped into the small cavern from outside, so all he could make out of her expression was the faint glimmer of her eyes as she turned to look at him.

He knew she couldn't see him in the dark, but he wondered what she'd seen earlier, at the hotel, when she'd looked at him. He'd let his hair grow in the year since he left the Army. Or maybe the better term was, he'd let it go. Like he'd let a lot of things go—his self-respect, his control over his temper, his once-upon-a-time ambitions. Even before taking on the role of the life-battered maintenance man, shuffling his way around the Highland Hotel and Resort, he'd been slacking off the simple disciplines of life, like shaving daily and trying to find a job that paid more than minimum wage.

Mostly, he'd wallowed. In self-pity. In anger. In a crushing amount of guilt for everything that had gone wrong for him since Afghanistan.

It had served his purposes to come across as a loser at the hotel. But if she could see him now, with the play-acting role sloughed off, would she see anything different?

He'd hoped this job with The Gates would give him back a sense of purpose. So far, all it had given him was a queasy sense of impending doom, a coming juggernaut of danger and disaster that left him feeling helpless and overwhelmed.

"Can I go?" Susannah asked quietly.

His gut tensed at the very thought. If she left this cave, she wasn't likely to reach civilization again without running into people who wanted her dead. She was a city girl, a pampered, polished princess who might know her way around a mall but had no chance getting out of these woods alive.

Nevertheless, he couldn't hold her captive. Not even for her own good. He'd been a prisoner once, and it had damn near destroyed him.

"Yes," he said quietly. "But I wouldn't, if I were you."

Her voice tightened. "Because there are people trying to kill me?"

"Yes."

"And how did you know they'd be there in the parking lot?"

He could hardly tell her that he was working with the people trying to kill her, but anything else was a lie or a secret he wasn't prepared to tell.

When he didn't answer immediately, her voice sharpened to a diamond edge. "Are you one of them?"

"You're still alive, aren't you?"

"That's not an answer."

"It's all you're gettin'." For now, at least, until they could reach someplace safe and contact Alexander Quinn.

She settled back into silence again, but she'd shifted far enough away from him that he knew any attempt to pull her back into the shelter of his arm would be seen as an assault, not an offer of comfort.

"It's raining," he said as the drumbeat of raindrops hitting the rocky ground outside filtered into the cave. "We're not going anywhere for the next little while, so why don't you try to grab a nap?"

Her voice rose. "You've got to be kidding me."

"Shh!" He slanted a quick look toward the cave entrance. Outside, the steady beat of rain masked almost all other noises. It would certainly cover any movement outside, which meant they were not only cornered with nowhere to run but also vulnerable to a sneak attack.

He'd tried to plan on the fly, once he'd learned the hit on Susannah Marsh had been moved up by twenty-four hours, but even faking illness to leave work early that afternoon had afforded him only a couple of hours to get his supplies together. He'd barely reached the parking lot in time to pull her pretty little bacon out of the fire.

"How do I even know there's anyone out there?" she asked, not bothering to lower her voice. "How do I know that wasn't just a car backfiring?"

She knew better. He could tell by the tension in her voice, the little tremble as her tone rose at the end of the question. She knew she was in danger, though he doubted she had any idea why. But she was also determined not to trust him one whit.

And he couldn't really blame her for that, could he, when he didn't even trust himself?

"You know it wasn't."

"I didn't get hit. They must have been lousy shots."

Fortunately, he was pretty sure they were. For one thing, they'd deliberately chosen to make the hit with pistols fired from a moving car, a piss-poor choice if you were serious about actually hitting your target. A critical thinker with any skills would have set up on the hill overlooking the parking lot with a Remington 700 or an AR-15 with a suppressor to keep down the noise.

Lucky for Susannah Marsh—and for him— they weren't dealing with critical thinkers.

But that didn't mean the men who were undoubtedly out there in the woods trying to track down their prey weren't dangerous as hell.

"There are a lot of them and only one of you," he said. "At close quarters, it won't matter if they're lousy shots."

"Who says they'll get close?" The volume of her voice dropped to a hiss of a whisper.

He almost laughed, trying to picture her out there in the woods, barefoot, dressed in a straight skirt that might make her legs look outstanding but wasn't ideal for hiking. The woman normally looked like a catalog model, all sparkling clean and perfectly groomed. He wouldn't be surprised if he turned on the flashlight right now to find that she'd somehow managed to finger-comb her hair back to its normal glossy state.

"So, you're not just a brilliant event planner but you're also an expert outdoorswoman?"

"You know nothing about me." She somehow made a whisper sound haughty.

He schooled the grin playing at the corners of his mouth. "I'll give you that."

A sharp noise outside sent animal awareness crackling along his nerves. He felt Susannah's instant tension snap across the space between them, as electric as lightning.

He reached out to touch her, to silently urge her to be quiet, and felt her skin ripple wildly beneath his touch. But she held her tongue as they waited in breathless agony for another noise.

The sound of footsteps barely registered above the hammering downpour of rain. Giving Susannah's arm a quick, reassuring squeeze, Hunter rose from the stone bench and moved toward the cave entrance, ignoring the protest of pain that clawed its way through his bum leg.

Keeping to the shadows just inside the cave, he looked out on the rain-drenched scene, letting his gaze relax. Movement would be easier to pinpoint if he wasn't actively looking for it.

There. He spotted a man dressed in dark camouflage moving slowly through the woods about twenty yards away. He held a pistol in one hand, a satellite phone in the other. It was hard to make out anything more about him through the heavy curtain of rain and mist, but from his general shape and size, Hunter guessed that the man outside the cave was probably Myron Abernathy, one of the handful of men Billy Dawson had directed to take down Susannah Marsh.

Myron had been one of the ones most enamored of her candid photo, Hunter remembered with a grimace. If he were to get her alone—

"Do you know him?" Susannah's taut whisper sent a shock wave rippling down his spine.

Taking a swift breath through his nose, he hissed, "Do you ever stay put when asked?"

"You didn't ask," she whispered back.

The urge to give her a shake was damn near overpowering. He allowed himself a quick glance in her direction, wishing there were more moonlight outside so he could get a better look at her expression.

But he didn't need moonlight to see that her eyes had widened and her perfectly shaped lips had trembled open with shock.

Following her gaze, he sucked in another sharp breath.

It was Myron Abernathy all right. No doubt about it.

Because he was ten yards closer and moving straight toward them.

Chapter Three

Oh God, oh God, oh G—

Hunter's hand closed over Susannah's mouth as a low, keening noise filled the tight confines of the cave. It took a second for her to realize the noise was coming from her own aching throat.

She swallowed the rest of the sound and moved backward with him, deeper into the shadows of the cave.

Outside, she could still hear the swishing noise of the man with the big gun moving through the thick underbrush and dead autumn leaves that carpeted the forest floor outside the cave. A few more steps and he'd—

A harsh bark of static made her jump. Hunter's arms tightened around her, as if he was trying to keep her from flying completely apart.

"Billy says regroup at the camp." A tinny voice, barely audible through the rain, floated into the cave.

Hunter's grip tightened like a spasm. Then she

heard the unmistakable sounds of the man outside retreating, moving steadily away from the mouth of the cave.

Hunter let her go, and she pulled away from him with a jerk, waiting until she could no longer hear the sound of movement outside before she asked in a low growl, "Who the hell is Billy?"

Hunter didn't answer. She hadn't expected he would. She was beginning to understand that silence meant he knew things he had no intention of telling her.

Like how he'd happened to be waiting in the parking lot at just the right time to play hero for her when the shooting started. Or how he happened to have an emergency kit packed and tucked away in his jacket, as if he wanted to be ready for whatever might go down tonight.

Or why there had been something hard poking into her ankle where his right leg had braced her when he pulled her back into his grasp.

He was armed. Ankle holster, which was why she hadn't spotted it before. Did that explain the limp? If he wasn't used to ankle-carry, he might not realize that unless he balanced the weapon with a counterweight on the other leg, like extra ammo strapped to the opposite ankle, it could seriously mess up his walking gait.

Except he limped with his left leg, didn't he? Not the leg with the weapon.

Before she had a chance to puzzle it out, Hunter snapped on the flashlight, slanting the beam across her face. She squinted, turning her face away from the painful glare. "Do you mind?"

"I do," he said, still speaking softly. "We got damn lucky just now. But you have got to learn to listen when I ask you to do something."

"You don't ask. You order," she muttered, kicking herself for saying anything at all. One of these days, her grandmother had always promised her, her smart mouth was going to get her into trouble.

As if it hadn't a million times already.

But fear made her angry, and abject terror made her furious *and* verbal about it. If Mr. Enigmatic Maintenance Man with the hidden gun and a hidden agenda couldn't handle a little pushback from her when he started barking orders, this night was about to go downhill at blazing speed.

"Look." He was struggling with some anger of his own. She could tell by the way his jaw was working, as if he had a mouth full of chew and no spit cup. "I know you're confused and scared. And I wish I could tell you there wasn't any reason to be, but we both know there is."

"I don't need you to candy-coat anything," she said flatly. "I just want to know all the facts. Why is somebody trying to kill me? And how did you know about it?" She swallowed the final question she wanted to ask, about the gun strapped to his ankle. It might be in her best interest to keep that knowledge to herself for the moment.

He gave her a long, considering look before he turned his gaze away, eyeing the narrow stone outcropping they'd used as a bench earlier. "I meant what I said about getting some sleep. It's cold and it's wet out there, and that gauze wouldn't last long if we started trekking through the woods tonight."

"It'll get torn up just as badly tomorrow."

"If you'll promise to sit tight and wait, I may have a way to fix that problem." He waved the flashlight beam toward the stone bench. "Get some sleep. I've got to go somewhere."

She stared at him, not believing what she was hearing. "You're going to leave me here? Alone?"

"They're convening somewhere else for the night. You should be safe enough." He didn't say it, but she could see the rest of what he was thinking in his hooded eyes. Even if he was here, there wouldn't be much they could do to hold off a whole crew of armed men looking to take her down. She wouldn't be much safer with him than stuck here shoeless with the damp, bitter cold and the rugged mountain terrain between her and safety.

"What are you going to do out there?"

He looked down at her bandaged feet. "Well, first of all, I'm going to get you some shoes." He lifted the flashlight upward again, handing it over to her. "You keep the light. I won't need it out there."

She closed her hand over the flashlight handle. It was warm where he'd gripped it, transferring welcome heat to her numb fingers.

But almost as soon as he slipped out into the rainy night, she extinguished the beam, preferring the comforting obscurity of the darkness to the stark reality the light revealed.

She was trapped and hunted. She was stuck with a man she didn't know, for reasons she wasn't sure she understood, in a place that might as well be the far side of the moon, for all the chance she had of finding her way out of these woods barefoot in the pouring rain.

Who was this man named Hunter? And why did his name seem to ring a bell with her, as if she'd heard it recently but couldn't quite place where? She'd certainly never seen him before, as far as she could remember, but there was still something about him that seemed familiar.

She made herself turn the light back on, aiming the beam around the small cave to get her bearings. Hunter hadn't told her where he was going, so she didn't know how long he might be away.

Bottom line, she did not need to spend the night in this cave with a man she didn't trust. If that meant wrapping her feet in every inch of gauze she could find in that first-aid kit he'd so kindly left with her, then that's what she had to do.

She had to get out of here before he got back, get to a safe place and start figuring out who those men with the guns really were.

Because if they were somehow connected to the Bradburys, then her life was about to get a thousand times more dangerous.

HUNTER DIDN'T THINK it was likely that Myron and the other boys had stumbled upon his hiding place while they'd been scouring the woods for any sign of Susannah Marsh. He'd stashed the large rucksack filled with emergency supplies in a hard-to-access area of the woods, where fallen trees and some rocky granite outcroppings created a natural nook perfect for hiding and sheltering something the size of the rucksack.

It was only slightly damp when he pulled it from its hiding place, and the water-resistant canvas lining would almost certainly have protected anything inside from the elements.

Not that he supposed Susannah Marsh would quibble about wet shoes; they'd certainly be a big improvement on the bloody gauze wrap currently protecting her battered feet.

He'd purchased a pair of hiking boots and another pair of tennis shoes he hoped would be comfortable for walking, though he wasn't exactly an expert on women's shoes. She had narrow, delicate-looking feet, although the hard calf and thigh muscles he'd seen—and felt—while carrying her through the woods on his back had suggested she wasn't nearly as soft and ornamental a woman as she looked.

That was good. She'd need to pull her weight over the next few days, until he could figure out what to do next.

He couldn't be sure Myron or the others had recognized him, but it was likely they had. So his undercover assignment was officially over, as far as he was concerned. While he suspected his boss might wish him to take a chance and try to get back inside the cell, he wasn't stupid enough to risk it. He'd already come damn close to pushing up daisies twice in his life.

No hurry to do that again anytime soon, right?

Hiking back to the cave with the backpack strapped to his shoulders reminded him of the frantic run through the woods with Susannah Marsh clinging to his back like a leech. A leech with long, well-toned legs and pert little breasts that had somehow managed to feel both soft and firm against his shoulder blades.

Plus, she'd smelled like freshly cut tart apples. How could she possibly have managed such a thing after a long day in the office and a headlong run for her life?

He tried to follow the path he and Susannah had taken earlier that night in hopes of tracking down his missing cell phone, but he'd seen no sign of the phone by the time he reached the cave entrance. He had to assume it was now in the custody of one of the Blue Ridge Infantry foot soldiers Billy Dawson had sent to kill Susannah Marsh.

The phone was a burner, and he took care not to leave any incriminating evidence for Dawson or the others to find. Even his calls to his handler, as he'd come to think of the wily old ex-spy who had hired him for this operation, were calls to another burner phone that would be next to impossible for Dawson and his crew to trace.

Alexander Quinn had made sure of that. After all, the Blue Ridge Infantry might be a crew of authority-hating rednecks with a mean streak, but not long ago, they'd aligned themselves with a band of tech-savvy anarchists as well as a hodgepodge of downright entrepreneurial drug cookers that had once formed the standing army for a criminal named Wayne Cortland.

Cortland had died a couple of years ago, and the authorities had largely dismantled the organization in a series of raids not long afterwards.

But the remaining remnants now had a blueprint for success. A business model, if you wanted to put it in those terms. When the local cops, already dealing with more than their share of crime, had moved on to other cases, Alexander Quinn had apparently decided to take up the slack. He seemed to be making the job of cleaning up the post-Cortland mess a personal project.

Overhead, a break in the rain clouds offered a brief glow of moonlight, just enough to reveal the rain-slick face of the rocky overhang that hid the small cave where Susannah Marsh was waiting. He slowed his approach, trying to prepare himself for telling her the truth about why he'd confronted her in the parking lot earlier that evening—and just what he had planned for them for the next few days.

She wasn't going to like it. That much he knew for sure. If Susannah Marsh was known for anything around the Highlands Hotel and Resort, it was her polished, professional look. Men and women alike commented on it when she wasn't in earshot, and not all of the talk was kind, but Hunter chalked the negative talk up to envy.

Susannah Marsh was damn near flawless. She dressed with meticulous style, her clothing a compromise between fashion and function. Never inappropriate, but always sleek and attractive. Perfectly groomed, perfectly competent, perfectly lovely.

But what he had in mind for the next few days, he was pretty sure she'd find perfectly appalling.

He had been sticking with a stealthy approach to the cave to this point, but he didn't want to sneak up on her and scare her, so as he reached the mouth of the cave, he made sure to make a little noise to give her notice of his arrival. "Susannah?" No answer.

Peering into the gloom, he tried to make out any signs of movement. But the cave interior was cold and still.

Pulling his keys from his pocket, he winced at the jingle of metal on metal as he located the small penlight he kept on his key chain. With a flick of his finger, the penlight beam came on, and he ran the light across the width of the cave.

The first-aid kit was still there, lying on the stone outcropping where they'd sat a little while earlier. Even the flashlight was there, snugged up next to the first-aid kit.

But Susannah Marsh was nowhere in sight.

The flashlight beam caught a glimmer of white on the cave floor beneath the stone bench. Crouching with a grimace of pain, he shined the light on the floor, taking in several half-moon-shaped white slivers. It took a second to realize what he was seeing.

Nail clippings. She'd cut off her nails.

He picked up the first-aid kit to put it in his pocket and stopped as he realized it was considerably lighter than when he'd used it to bandage her feet earlier. When he checked inside, he found that all of the gauze that had been packed within was gone.

What the hell was the woman up to?

Was she crazy to be doing this?

When Susannah had left the cave, she'd been certain that the worst possible choice she could make was to stay there and wait for Hunter to get back. No matter how attractive he might seem, especially when he was standing between her and a bunch of men with guns, he wasn't her friend. He wasn't even an acquaintance. He was just a guy she'd seen for the first time in an elevator earlier that very day. For all she knew, he'd been lying when he told her he'd hit the button for the wrong floor.

Maybe he'd been looking for her the whole time.

But now that she was out in the woods, shivering from the cold and biting her lip to keep from moaning over the pain in her injured feet, she was beginning to second-guess her decision to strike out on her own.

Yes, she knew a little something about getting around in the mountains. And yes, she'd done a pretty damn good job of fashioning shoes out of gauze, tape and a couple of slabs of wood she'd used her Swiss Army knife to shave off a fallen tree limb she'd found near the mouth of the cave.

But the makeshift shoes were already starting to fall apart, no match for the wet, tangled underbrush and rocky soil. The temperature had to have dropped another five or ten degrees since sunset, and her coat was made for getting from the office to the car, not for traipsing around in the woods on a cold, damp October night.

And worst of all, she had a bad feeling she was lost.

She usually could find her way around anywhere, but in her panic to get away from men shooting at her, she'd lost track of what direction they'd gone. She'd never learned to navigate by the stars, having grown up in the middle of the Smoky Mountains, a long way from the sea. And the heavens had opened up again, anyway, mountain fog and driving rain obscuring everything outside a fifty-yard radius.

She might as well be in the middle of a big, tree-strewn void for all the good her surroundings were doing her at the moment.

Stubbornly quelling the panic starting to hurtle up from her trembling gut, she made herself stop and take a long, deep breath. *Look around. What do you see?*

Trees. Fog.

Someone moving through the woods ahead.

Shock zapped through her, compelling her to run. She clamped down on the instinct, knowing that movement was the worst possible thing at the moment. Standing very still, several yards from the dark silhouettes she could barely make out moving through the mist about thirty yards away, she had a chance to escape their notice. Her coat was a dark olive-green trench that covered her from neck to knee, and the underbrush covered her legs from toes to knees. Only her face and hands would be visible in the damp gloom, and they might be mistaken for the patchy white trunk of a birch tree.

As long as she stayed very, very still.

Nearby, something rustled in the underbrush. She held her position, ruthlessly suppressing the urge to turn her head and see what was moving around so close by.

Ahead, the two dark-clad figures walking through the trees kept moving. Apparently they'd heard nothing, or if they had, they'd chalked it up to an animal wandering around in the rain.

The pounding rush of her pulse in her ears was

so loud it almost eclipsed the staccato beat of the rain, which had risen to a torrent. Even the thick evergreen boughs overhead weren't enough to keep her from becoming thoroughly drenched. But she didn't move, not even to wipe the rain out of her stinging eyes.

The dark figures kept moving, gliding with terrifying silence through the fog until they disappeared from her sight.

She ignored her body's urge to crumple into a boneless heap and stayed still a few moments longer until she was sure the prowling men were no longer in earshot.

She heard the rustling noise again. Closer this time.

Her patience and control left in a snap, and she started running headlong through the woods, heedless of the noise she was making or the painful slap of her unraveling gauze-and-tape footwear against her battered feet. All she could think about was the chill-inducing menace of the men she'd seen gliding through the misty woods like vengeful ghosts.

The tape on her right foot tore away completely, and she went sprawling, barely catching herself from landing face-first on the rocky ground. She hit hard, the impact driving the air from her lungs and leaving her gasping and heaving for breath.

For a few terrifying seconds, the world around her seemed to go completely black as her oxygen-starved lungs struggled to refill. And in that frightening void, Susannah heard her grandmother's voice, sharp and clear.

"Get yourself together, girl. Ain't nobody gonna fix your troubles 'cept you."

Air seeped into her lungs, easing the blackness. Cold, damp air replaced the burning pain in her chest, and slowly her pulse descended from the stratosphere to a fast but steady cadence.

Get yourself together, girl, she repeated silently, gathering up the remains of her ersatz shoe and examining it to see if there was any hope of making a repair.

Nope. It was a goner.

Allowing herself only a second or two of despair, she rose to her feet and shoved the bundle of tattered gauze and tape in the pocket of her flimsy jacket. Gingerly putting her injured foot on the ground, she gauged the discomfort level and, while it hurt like hell, she thought she could bear it, at least a little while longer.

She took a careful step forward. The ground was rough, wet and hard, but she could take it.

The flurry of movement behind her came out of thick silence, like a whirlwind born from dead calm. She had time to suck in a quick breath and take a stumbling step forward before she was jerked back against a wall of hard heat. A large hand clamped over her mouth and a low drawl rumbled in her ear.

"Don't make a sound."

Chapter Four

He could feel her heartbeat against his chest, fluttering like a frantic bird. Not daring to unclamp his hand from her mouth, he whispered in her ear, "It's Hunter. I know you saw those men out there. You need to stop making so damn much noise."

He felt her body tense up, her muscles knotting as she strained against his grip. He tightened his hold and added, "If I let you go, will you promise not to scream?"

Slowly, she nodded.

He eased his grip, watching for any sign that she wasn't going to keep her promise. She jerked free of his grasp and whirled around to look at him, her eyes blazing in the watery glint of moonlight peeking through the storm clouds overhead. "Who were they?" Her words came out so softly, he saw more than heard the question.

He put one finger over his lips and turned away from her, reaching both hands over his shoulders toward her. With a soft exhalation, she caught his hands and he hauled her onto his back, releasing her hands once she had a firm grip on his shoulders and wrapping his arms around her legs to hold her safely in place.

"This is humiliating, you know," she whispered in his ear, her breath stirring his hair and sending a shudder of raw masculine need scudding down his spine. He closed his eyes, took a long, slow breath and let it out in a ten count. Then he started back through the woods the way he'd come, hoping the rainfall would obscure their trail before anyone came back out here to start looking for them again.

He'd stashed his supplies between a couple of large boulders, hidden under a dun-colored rain tarp, in case someone discovered the cave before he got back. Carrying them in his backpack had made sense when he thought they'd have time for a more leisurely escape. But it was a whole other thing to chase an escapee through the woods while dodging unidentified strangers carrying a heavy pack on his back.

He stopped by the pair of boulders and set her down.

"Why are we stopping?" she whispered.

"For this." He tugged the tarpaulin from over the large rucksack, folding it neatly and handing it to her.

She stared at the large olive-drab backpack first, then at him. "How long were you planning this?" Even though she still spoke in a whisper, her inflection rose, and he could see in the widening of her eyes that she found his foresight alarming.

"This particular set of circumstances?" he answered quietly, slinging one strap of the pack over his shoulder. "About three hours."

She eyed him nervously as he held out his free arm. "You knew there were going to be people gunning for me tonight, didn't you?"

He didn't see the point of dissembling. "Yes."

"How?"

"Let's get back in the cave and see how much damage you did to my handiwork." He didn't wait for her to make a move. He just wrapped his arm around her, lifting her half off her feet, and started walking toward the cave.

He hadn't given her much choice but to stumble along beside him. Considering the flaring anger he could practically see swirling around her like a big red cloud, he was grateful she didn't show any signs of fighting him as he hauled her into the cave.

He should have known he wasn't going to get away with the caveman act for long. The second he let her go and turned to set the rucksack down on the floor of the cave, she sucker punched him right in the kidney.

Pain exploded through his side, shooting off shrapnel of pure agony to tear through his gut and groin. Doubling over, he wheeled to fend off her next blow, but it never came. When the stars cleared from his vision, he found himself staring into her crumpled face.

The damn woman was crying.

Before he could process the unexpected sight, she'd regained control, her expression returning to a cool, neutral mask as she dashed away the tears from her eyes as if they were mere raindrops that had slithered down from her damp hair.

"Think you could answer a question directly now?" she asked in a regal tone that sent ice flooding his veins.

There was the princess he knew.

"You gonna sucker punch me again if I don't?"

Her mask slipped, just a bit, a hint of a wry smile hovering over the corners of her lips. The rain had washed away her carefully applied makeup, leaving her bedraggled and natural, but she still looked utterly royal and in control. "If necessary."

He rubbed his back over the site of her blow. The skin was tender, but the worst of the pain had ebbed to a dull ache. "You went for the kidney."

"Shameful of me." She didn't sound particularly regretful, but he'd seen that moment of breakdown, no matter how quickly she'd managed to don the icy mask again.

"I was working with them. But I wasn't one of them." He hadn't meant to tell her even that much, but the second he opened his mouth, the words had spilled in a rush.

Her eyes narrowing, she nodded toward the backpack he'd dropped when she hit him. "Did you put the flashlight in there?"

"Yeah."

She bent to pick up the pack, grunting a little as she encountered the unexpected weight. "How long did you pack for?"

"A few days. More if we can get to a place where we can do some laundry."

She located the flashlight he'd tucked in one of the pack's outer pockets and flicked on the switch. Light knifed through the darkness, piercing Hunter right in the eyes.

"You planned to kidnap me." It wasn't a question, and her tone was oddly neutral, as if she were merely a disinterested observer trying to make sense of a situation she'd stumbled upon.

"I knew I'd have to get you away from that parking lot, yes."

"Because of the gunmen."

He hadn't really been sure exactly how they

planned to kill her. Guns had seemed a reasonable option, since most of the men in the cell owned them. A whole carload of them shooting off their guns and making a lot of noise hadn't exactly been what he'd been expecting, though. The concept of stealth apparently didn't factor into how the BRI conducted their business.

Calling themselves an "infantry," he thought with a grimace. They weren't fit to lick the boots of the real warriors they claimed to emulate.

She must have seen the grimace. "You weren't expecting the gunmen?"

"I wasn't sure what to expect. I only knew that whatever they had planned was happening this evening, and I had to get you out of there."

She looked at him for a long, silent moment, then walked slowly over to the stone bench and sat. It was a little high and narrow to make a proper bench, forcing her to perch more than sit. She looked bone-tired and disheartened, and one of her feet, the one that had lost whatever crazy bandage she'd put on them for her trek through the woods, was bleeding again.

At least he could help her out with that.

He picked up the pack she'd set down on the cave floor and unzipped the main compartment. The beam of the flashlight slanted toward him, and he made a show of letting her see what he was doing. "I packed some shoes for you. I figured you'd be in heels, and they're not exactly made for wandering around the woods."

"You don't know my size."

She'd be surprised what he knew. Like the fact that she kept a pair of tennis shoes in her desk drawer in case she wanted to do a power walk during her lunch hour. Or her secret addiction to dark-chocolate drops. It was remarkable how many secrets a maintenance man could uncover if he was interested enough to snoop around while doing his work.

She kept her desk and belongings more neat and inscrutable than most, but he'd been able to get her foot size from the running shoes. He'd have preferred to sneak out her actual shoes, but there'd been no chance to slip into the office that afternoon before the trouble started going down. He'd had to make a run into Barrowville to do some shopping at the thrift store in town.

Deciding on the tennis shoes over the hiking boots, he tossed them to the cave floor in front of her and kept digging for the sweater and jeans he'd bought at the same thrift store. The sweater would fit, even if it was a little big. The jeans looked as if they'd fit as well, although he might have to come up with something to use as a belt.

Susannah picked up the shoes and looked inside at the size. Her gaze snapped up to meet his, her lips tight with dismay. "Have you been stalking me? Is that what this is really about?"

He almost laughed at the thought. If she only knew how much he wished he was pretty much anywhere else but here at the moment—

"Don't suppose you have a phone stashed in there?" she asked a moment later when he didn't reply.

"Sorry. No." He found the sweater and jeans and carried them over to her. She looked at the garments through narrow, suspicious eyes. "They're warmer," he said bluntly.

"How long do you plan to keep me out here?" She didn't reach for the clothes.

With a shrug, he set the clothes on the stone bench beside her. "At least forty-eight more hours."

She turned her gaze from the clothes to him. "Why forty-eight hours?"

He waited for her to figure it out.

Her eyes snapped open wider. "This is about the conference this weekend?"

He pulled one last item from the pack, a corduroy jacket. It wouldn't be heavy enough if the temperature really dropped over the next few days, but it should be enough, with the sweater and jeans, to ward off hypothermia during their hike out of this part of the mountain.

He set it on top of the other clothes. "I'm going

outside for a few minutes to scout around, see if there's any sign of those other men we saw a little while ago. Go ahead and get dressed. We don't have a lot of time."

"Don't have a lot of time for what?" she asked, not making a move toward the clothes.

He tried not to lose his patience, knowing it was a lot to ask of her to wait for events to unfold when she was cold, injured and probably scared out of her pretty wits. "We need to leave this cave and go somewhere safer and warmer."

"Like a police station?"

He didn't even roll his eyes that time. Improvement.

But he didn't bother to answer her question before he walked out into the rainy night.

HE MIGHT BE a frustrating cipher, but the man knew how to pick warm and comfortable clothes, Susannah had to concede a few minutes later as she tugged a thick corduroy jacket over the fuzzy sweater. He'd chosen clothing a little larger than her size, but his spot-on choice of footwear suggested he'd opted for the larger size deliberately, figuring it would be easier to get around in roomy clothing than a tighter fit. The jeans were a notch too large, but not so big that she needed a belt, thanks to her stress-induced chocolate binge over the past week.

He was waiting outside the cave, his sharp green eyes scanning the misty woods. He seemed to take his sentry duty very seriously, making her wonder what, exactly, he used to do for a living before taking a job as a hotel maintenance worker.

Clearly there was more to the man than she'd assumed. His earlier show of shy deference was long gone, replaced by a stubborn implacability that was somehow both unnerving and comforting.

"Any sign of intruders?" she asked quietly.

He answered without looking at her. "No. But we can't assume they're not out there."

"So we hike out of here, anyway?"

"Something like that."

She shifted from one foot to the other, testing the feel of the shoes on her injured feet. He'd included a pair of thick, fluffy socks that padded her wounds well enough, but they made the shoes a tighter fit than she might have liked.

On the other hand, the tight fit offered good arch support, which she'd probably appreciate if they were planning to hike their way out of these woods.

Unfortunately, she realized a half hour later, leaving the woods didn't seem to be part of the plan. They were headed into deeper forest, on a winding but unmistakable upward climb. The mist thickened, but the air thinned. They were heading higher into the mountains, which meant they were going east.

She might not be a geographer, but she knew that Barrowville and civilization lay to the west. "We're not heading out of the woods, are we?"

He didn't look at her. It seemed to be a habit with him. "I have a cabin about two miles from here. Not much, but it's warm and there's food and water there."

"You want us to hike two more miles tonight?"

"If we wait until morning, there'll be cops and searchers swarming this area looking for you."

"You're not exactly providing me a good reason to go with you."

"Well, how about this? I know there's at least one cop on the take in Barrowville, which has jurisdiction in this area. I just don't know who he is. Or what he looks like."

"And I have to take your word for that?" she countered sharply. "Because you've given me such a good reason to trust you up to this point."

"I saved you from being mowed down in the hotel parking lot." His voice was razor-edged. "I brought you clothes to warm you up and shoes to protect your feet. Hell, I carried you piggyback. Twice. And let me tell you, princess, you may not be an Amazon, but you're not exactly dainty, either."

She faltered to a stop, shooting him a dark look. "Clearly, you're not looking to impress me with your gentlemanly charms, either."

He laughed, turning to look at her for the first time since they'd left the cave. "I'm a lot of things, darlin', but a gentleman ain't one of them."

As he started hiking forward again, she caught up and asked, "Does the cabin have indoor plumbing?"

She saw the slight curve of his lips but he didn't answer her question, pushing forward at a surprising clip, given his obvious limp.

Gritting her teeth against the pain of her injured feet, she hurried up the mountain after him.

THE CABIN WAS, to put it mildly, rustic. It had running water and electricity, but that was the extent of luxuries his little bolt-hole could offer, and during the winter, when the snows fell, electricity wasn't a given.

He had a woodstove for the long, cold nights when the power failed, and a rainwater cistern if a pipe burst from the occasional deep freeze. Canned goods in the pantry could be opened by hand and heated over the woodstove.

It wasn't Highland Hotel and Resort, and he doubted Susannah Marsh would find much to please her refined tastes, but she wouldn't freeze and she wouldn't starve. Considering how close she'd come to bleeding out in the hotel employees' parking lot, she'd have to make do, at least until he figured out what to do next.

Contacting Quinn directly was out, at least for the moment, even though he had another burner phone stashed in the cabin. His second call to his boss that afternoon had gone straight to voice mail, a preordained signal that Quinn suspected their line of communication might be compromised.

Hunter didn't know what constituted "compromised communication," but he knew better than to doubt the instincts of his wily boss. Quinn might be borderline paranoid, but he'd managed to survive some of the most hair-raising covert ops in history. Survival skills like those meant something, even to a former Army infantry grunt like Hunter, who'd never cared much for the spooks who'd haunted the perimeters of the battlefield during major military ops.

He might not ever really like Quinn, but he trusted the man's finely honed sense of caution.

They veered off the barely visible path as they neared the hidden cabin. Behind him, Susannah was still struggling to keep up with his long strides, though she walked with less noise than he'd expected. It was taking sheer determination on his own part to maintain as much stealth as possible, because his old war wounds were hurting like hell.

The clearing appeared almost without warning, with no discernible path to announce its existence. A ring of firs, pines and hemlocks stood sentinel around the tiny homestead, protecting the cabin from view even in the winter, when hardwood trees would shed their leaves for the season. The evergreens had been planted there nearly a half century earlier by his grandfather, who'd preferred seclusion to the increasingly dangerous world outside.

Catching up as Hunter slowed his gait, Susannah sucked in a small gasp of air, and he wondered idly what she thought of the place.

The cabin wasn't much to look at from the outside, a low-slung edifice built from rough-hewn logs. The porch extended along the whole front of the cabin, but it wasn't very wide because the cabin wasn't large.

Two steps up and they were at the front door.

Because of its seclusion, there had never been any reason to put in a lock, and for decades, the door had remained unlocked and the cabin undisturbed. But Hunter didn't see the point of taking chances, not after how easily he'd been ambushed and abducted several months ago. He'd installed a sturdy padlock on both the front and back doors of the cabin, and new latches on all the windows.

He saw Susannah eyeing those latches as he led her into the cabin and turned the dead bolt behind them. Probably thought he was keeping her prisoner, and he didn't hurry to disabuse her of the idea. If a little healthy fear would keep her from doing something foolish, like trying to sneak off on her own again, then he'd use it.

"Nice place," she said. Her tone wasn't obviously sarcastic, but he assumed she meant the comment that way.

He knew the place wasn't much, but it offered him a sense of security in an increasingly insane world. It was one of the few things he owned that he hadn't sold to raise his sister's bail money.

"I know it doesn't look very big, but there's a good-size bedroom. You can have it, of course. I'll take the couch."

He saw her eye the old sofa with skepticism, and he couldn't really blame her. He'd bought the battered piece of furniture at the thrift store in Barrowville a few months earlier, but for all its shabby appearance, the springs were sturdy enough and the cushions comfortable, even though his legs hung off a bit when he slept there.

He'd stayed in the cabin several times since returning home from Afghanistan, when his guilt about his sister's legal troubles had gotten to be too much for him to cope with back at her place. He'd bunked down here on the sofa more often than not, finding its rougher embrace easier to deal with than the civilized softness of the bed.

"How can you be sure I won't sneak out while you're asleep?" she asked quietly as he dropped the rucksack on the low coffee table and began to unpack supplies.

He slanted a look toward her. "You're not my prisoner."

"Forgive me if I feel that way."

He waved his hand toward the door. "You know how dead bolts work. Feel free to let yourself out."

She actually took a couple of steps toward the door before she stopped, her chin dipping to her chest. Not looking at him, she asked, "Why were they trying to kill me?"

There was a strange undertone to her question that piqued his curiosity, as if she already knew the answer but needed him to say the words aloud.

So he did. "You're in the way of their plan."

Her gaze flickered up to meet his, confusion glittering in her eyes. He saw with a jolt of surprise that one of her brown eyes had gone light gray with a touch of hazel around the pupil. He blinked a couple of times before he was sure what he was seeing.

"What?" she asked, noticing his reaction.

"You wear brown contacts."

Her brow furrowing, she blinked a couple of times herself. "Damn."

"Why would you want to hide your eye color?" he blurted.

She looked down. "I like variety."

She was lying.

"You didn't finish answering my question," she continued, her gaze stubbornly averted. "I'm in the way of what plan?"

He might as well tell her, he supposed. If anyone had a right to know what was going on, it was the woman who'd damn near given up her life for what the BRI had planned.

"A militia group called the Blue Ridge Infantry is planning to sabotage the law enforcement convention being held at the hotel this weekend."

Chapter Five

"Why?"

The question spilled from Susannah's lips before she had time to formulate a rational thought. If she had, she might have asked a more important question, such as how he knew these things and how the attack was supposed to take place.

But she supposed "why" was a good start.

Especially since her cousin McKenna was going to be one of the attendees.

Another question popped into her head. Could the Bradburys have made the connection between Susannah and her cousin? Had they targeted the upcoming conference knowing McKenna was going to be there?

Wouldn't that be ironic? Targeting the conference because of McKenna, never realizing that Susannah herself was right there in the thick of it all.

But the Bradburys had never been connected to any militia groups, had they? They'd always been freakishly clannish, prone to trusting no-body but family, however vile and revolting those kinsmen might be.

Hunter's growl of a voice interrupted her mus-ings. "Two hundred top cops from three states in one hotel? Hell of a temptation to a bunch of people who loathe authority." He waved toward the sofa, a tacit invitation to have a seat.

She limped to the sofa and sat on one end, sur-prised to find the piece of furniture sturdier and more comfortable than it looked. She glanced up at him, putting aside the thoughts of her cousin and any possible connection to the Bradburys of Boneyard Ridge. Sometimes coincidences were just coincidences.

"And you're part of the plan?" she asked.

"I was what you'd call a forward scout, I sup-pose." He answered with his back to her, crossing to the fireplace that took up half the near wall. But instead of logs, a large space heater filled the width of the fireplace. He plugged it in to the wall socket and a few seconds later, the unit hissed to life, giving off blessed heat and ambient light.

"What do you do for heat when the power's out?" she asked.

He glanced at her. "There's a woodstove in the bedroom and another one in the kitchen. But the lines to this place were laid underground, so there aren't as many outages as you might expect from a place this far up the mountain."

"How did you ever find this place?"

"My grandfather built it. Let's just say, he lived through the early years of the Cold War and prepared for any eventuality." He smiled, but behind the humor, she saw a hint of admiration as well. He seemed to be a man who appreciated the benefits of having a good contingency plan.

Military, she thought after a moment's consideration, remembering the rucksack full of necessary supplies. Not one of those desk-jockey rear-echelon types, either. She tried to picture his hair, currently collar-length and wavy, cut in a crisp, military style. What did they call it, high and tight?

She could see it, she decided, her gaze narrowing as it skimmed the hard angle of his jaw. Could explain the bum leg as well.

Something flitted in the back of her mind, tantalizingly out of reach. Something to do with a wounded warrior—

"No more questions?" he asked, jerking her attention back to her present situation.

"Why me?"

"I told you. You were in the way."

"Of what? I'm not in security."

His gaze flicked her way. "Yeah, I know."

"What was your role? Following me around? Is

that why you stayed on the elevator earlier today instead of getting off?"

His lips curved slightly at the corners, carving shallow dimples in his lean cheeks. "No, that was my own bit of freelancing."

"I suppose you're going to tell me you're really on my side."

The dimples deepened, though there wasn't much in the way of mirth shining from his green eyes. "I suppose you wouldn't believe me if I did."

"I don't know," she admitted, then immediately wished she'd just kept her mouth shut. She was in a very vulnerable situation at the moment, and showing any sign of weakness in front of this man was just asking for trouble.

If her grandmother had taught her anything during the long, hard years of her childhood, it was to never show weakness. Displays of weakness made you look like a tasty morsel for the big, bad wolves of the world, and in the neck of the woods where she'd grown up, there were a whole hell of a lot of nasty wolves roaming those hills and hollows.

She knew from personal experience.

"I don't want anyone hurt. But whatever they're planning for the conference is only the opening act. And I'm not sure what they have in mind for the main event."

Though she wasn't a hundred percent confident that he was telling her the truth about where his loyalties lay, he clearly wanted her to believe he was one of the good guys. So for now, she'd play into that conceit, she decided. What she needed most at the moment was more information, and she'd get it more easily with cooperation than conflict. "What you did for me blew your cover, didn't it?"

He released a long, gusty breath. "I'm not sure."

"They were pretty close when they started shooting."

"They consider me a loser. It's why they didn't let me in on all their plans." He turned to look at her. "You almost didn't recognize me out there yourself, did you? And you were a hell of a lot closer."

She hadn't, she realized. Not at first. Of course, she didn't exactly know him well. "I take it you like for them to think you're not much of a threat."

"It served my purposes," he agreed. "If there's one way they're akin to a real military unit, it's that the people in charge like to make sure there are plenty of warm bodies out there as cannon fodder while they plot world domination from the rear."

Yup, she thought, former military. And not

a big fan of authority himself. She filed that thought away and turned her gaze toward the glow of the space heater. Her feet felt as if they'd swollen to twice their normal size, and she didn't look forward to putting her weight on them anytime soon, but the lure of heat proved too powerful. Nibbling her lip to keep from whimpering, she hobbled over to the fireplace and outstretched her hands toward the heater.

Hunter stepped out of her view, and it took all her willpower not to turn and watch where he went. But the whole point of this cooperative captive thing was to convince him it was safe to let down his guard.

She heard the scrape of wood against wood, and then Hunter's big, warm hand flattened against her spine, sending shock waves rippling through her flesh. Clenching her jaw to control her body's helpless reaction, she turned and found him eyeing her, his expression wary. He gestured with his free hand toward the ladderback kitchen chair he'd retrieved for her. "Sit down. Let me take a better look at your feet."

She sat as he asked, curling her fingers around the edge of the chair seat when he picked up one foot and propped it on his knee.

"May I?" He met her narrowed gaze before nodding toward her foot.

She nodded briskly, and he untied her shoelaces, easing the sneaker from her foot. Her feet had definitely swelled a bit, if the painfully tight fit of the shoe was anything to go by. The socks he'd provided were stained in places, sticking to her foot here and there where blood had dried. But she barely felt any pain, her nerve endings focused entirely on the light rasp of his work-roughened fingers against her bare skin.

He winced a little as he tugged the fabric away from a particularly large scrape. "Sorry."

She took the chance to tug her feet away. "I can take it from here."

He left the front room, disappearing somewhere into the darkened back of the cabin and returning a short time later with a wet washcloth. He handed it over, and she gasped a little at the coldness of the water.

"Sorry. It takes a bit for the water heater to kick in, and I didn't want to make you wait. Warm it a minute in front of the heater if it's too cold."

She didn't wait, welcoming the sharp bite of the cold cloth on her skin as a necessary distraction from her body's troubling response to his touch. The last thing she needed to do was get sucked into some stupid Stockholm-syndrome crush on the man who was, for all intents and purposes, her captor.

No matter how sexy he looked when he watched her with those smoldering green eyes.

He passed her a tube of antibiotic ointment when she'd finished washing the scrapes and cuts on her feet. "Want me to make sure you got all the dirt out of those wounds?"

She shook her head quickly and took the ointment. "I'm good." She slathered the ointment over the abrasions, rebandaged her feet and took the clean pair of socks he offered. "Thanks."

He settled back on his haunches, looking up at her through narrowed eyes the color of the Atlantic in winter, somewhere between green and gray. "I know you're scared," he said in a low, gravelly tone that scattered goose bumps along her arms. "I won't let anyone find you here. I promise."

Pretend you trust him. Get him to drop his guard.

She forced a smile. "Thank you."

He gazed at her for a long, unnerving moment before his lips curved at the corners and those incongruous dimples appeared in his lean, hard face. "I'll go get the heater in the bedroom cranked up so you'll be nice and toasty. Sit here a while longer and thaw out."

She watched him until he disappeared through the door that led somewhere in the back of the small cabin. Releasing a gusty breath, she looked into the glowing wires of the heater and willed her trembling limbs to stillness. She wanted to believe him, she realized with alarm. She wanted the warmth and kindness she'd heard in his voice to be real.

But it couldn't be. Even if he was telling her the truth, he had his own agenda and it had nothing to do with her. She'd be a fool to trust her life to him or anyone else.

If she'd learned anything in the last twelve years, it was that the only person she could depend on was herself.

SHE WAS GOING to run again. Hunter didn't think it would be tonight, not after her close call in the woods. She might even bide her time here for a day or two, let her battered feet mend a bit more. Learn a little about the lay of the land, take time to formulate an actual plan, rather than act on impulse.

But she was going to make a break for it, sooner or later.

She wasn't the pampered princess he'd thought she was. That much was certain.

But what, exactly, was she? Why was she hiding those gorgeous hazel-tipped gray eyes behind contacts? Why had he spotted in her dusky hair hints of blond roots gleaming like gold in the firelight?

And those scars he'd spotted, barely visible on her smooth, shapely legs, weren't razor nicks. They were evidence of a hard-knock childhood spent doing things like climbing trees and skinning her knees and shins on rocks and roots.

So, a tomboy. And a mountain girl, too. Her accent was almost neutral, her vocabulary sophisticated, but he'd caught a hint here and there of her Appalachian roots.

And if he retained any capacity for reading people, the woman was hiding something. Something big. Important.

Life-threatening?

He wished he could get in touch with Quinn, but until he received some sort of all-clear signal, he had to assume that his available lines of communication were compromised. Ever since Quinn had involved himself in the currently dormant investigation of the Blue Ridge Infantry, the former spook had become downright paranoid about infiltration.

A few weeks on the ground with the BRI had convinced Hunter that his boss was probably giving the ragtag band of soldier wannabes and washed-out former grunts a lot more credit for cohesion and strategic planning than they deserved.

But maybe Quinn knew something Hunter didn't. Hunter had been in the Army long enough to realize that sometimes in a war, the soldiers on the ground could see only part of a larger strategy playing out across a wide and varied battlefield.

Maybe Billy Dawson and his crew weren't the tip of the BRI spear.

Maybe they were the distraction.

The hiss of the space heater near the bed wasn't loud enough to mask the sounds of movement coming from the front room. For a second, his gut tightened as he feared he'd miscalculated the strength of her desire to get away from him, and he was halfway out of the room before he recognized what he was hearing.

She was turning on the lamps in the front room. He could hear the soft clicks of the power knobs turning. Even from here, he could see the glow of the lamp bulbs as they flicked on, one after another.

He supposed she'd had about all the darkness this evening she could stand.

He had, too, he thought, reaching for the bedroom light switch and flicking on the light.

He looked the room over with a critical eye. He hadn't had time to do more than neaten the place up before he'd had to head back to the hotel in hopes of getting her out of harm's way before Billy's men struck.

He heard footsteps approaching down the hallway, and he steeled himself for her appearance as he turned toward the doorway.

She stopped in the portal, looking past him briefly to take in the particulars of the room before turning her sharp eyes to him. She'd removed the other brown contact lens, he saw, receiving the full impact of those cool gray-hazel eyes.

He blurted the first thing that came to mind. "Fresh sheets."

Her lips curved slightly. "Good to know."

Well, now he felt like an idiot.

"Where's the bathroom?"

"The door you passed to get here."

"Thanks."

"I guess I'll go, then."

She gave a little nod and watched him all the way in as he closed the distance between them, edging around her in the tight space between the bed and the door. Her body radiated heat and the lingering green-apple scent that had haunted him all afternoon, ever since he'd shared the elevator with her earlier.

Everything about this whole damn mission had gone belly-up, he thought as he rode a wave of frustration and testosterone into the cabin's small front room. And he had no idea how to fix it.

But he'd better figure it out, and soon. Because this cabin might be well-hidden and reasonably well-fortified, but if the authorities weren't already searching these woods for the pretty young event planner who'd just gone missing, they'd be crawling these hills by morning.

And they were the lesser of the two evils who'd be looking for them.

Settling on the sofa, he reached into his battered rucksack and pulled a slim leather wallet from a pocket hidden deep inside the pack. Flipping it open, he gazed at the photo tucked inside the first clear plastic sleeve. It had been taken almost a decade ago, just before his first tour of duty. His sister, Janet, and her husband, Dale, had driven to Georgia to see him off, and Dale had snapped a picture of Hunter and his older sister, all three of them aware it might be the last day they'd ever spend together.

They'd been right. But it hadn't been Hunter who'd left the others behind. It had been his brother-in-law, who'd passed away from a burst aneurysm a year into Hunter's two-year tour of duty, leaving Janet alone to pick up the pieces of her shattered life.

Hunter could have left the Army when his enlistment ended, but he hadn't. By then, Janet had seemed to be recovering from her loss, working a new job in the county prosecutor's office.

And Hunter had liked the Army, liked the camaraderie and the discipline, things he and his sister had lacked growing up with a good-hearted but soft-willed mother who'd been little more than a child herself. Hunter had never known his father, and even Janet had only fuzzy memories of the man who'd left when she was just four years old. And their mother had died in a car accident shortly after his sixteenth birthday.

For a long time, it had been just the two of them. She'd been part sister, part mother to him for most of his life, but when she'd needed him most, he'd let her down.

He had to figure out some way to make things up to her. He'd hoped his work with The Gates was going to be an answer, but he'd already blown his first assignment. What were the odds Alexander Quinn would ask him back for a second?

Footsteps on the hardwood floor behind him gave him a brief warning. He closed the wallet and turned to look at Susannah Marsh standing in the doorway.

"Is there anything to eat around here?" she asked.

He pushed to his feet. "Of course. Yes."

He had to pass her to get to the kitchen situated at the very back of the cabin. It was one of the cabin's roomier areas, large enough to accommodate a table near the back door and an old gas stove and oven. The refrigerator was small but still kept things cold and the freezer unit kept things frozen. He wasn't sure how much longer all the original appliances would stay useful, but for now, they served the purpose.

"Want something hot?"

"Soup would be fine," she said with a smile he didn't quite buy.

He'd stocked the pantry a while back, long before he'd known he'd be working for The Gates. He'd figured on using the cabin as a place to get away sometimes, to hide from a world that had become alien to him in so many ways. The cabin had belonged to Janet, who'd inherited it from their mother when she died. Janet had handed over the keys to Hunter when he returned home after his injury.

He supposed she'd known that he'd need a place to hunker down sometimes. To lick his wounds in private.

He doubted she'd ever thought he'd be using it to practically keep a woman prisoner.

"I wish I could let you contact your family," he said.

"Let me?" She shot him a look that stung.

"Bad choice of words," he conceded. "I wish it was safe."

"It doesn't matter. Nobody to contact, anyway."

He frowned. "Nobody will notice you've gone missing? I don't believe that."

"No family to contact," she said with a shrug, looking through the freestanding pantry. "People at work will notice, of course. Especially this close to the upcoming conference…." Her voice trailed off, and her gaze rose toward the ceiling. "Do you hear that?"

Hunter listened. At first, he heard only the sound of wind whistling around the cabin's eaves, and the faint whisper of rain drizzle. But slowly, the deep, rhythmic *whump-whump* sound of spinning rotors filtered through the ambient noise.

"Helicopter," he said quietly, his gut tightening.

"Looking for me?"

"I don't know." He reached over and turned off the kitchen light, then headed through the house and extinguished the rest.

"They'll find this place eventually." Susannah's voice was so close behind him he could feel her breath on his neck. "Won't they?"

"Probably," he admitted.

But he couldn't let it happen tonight.

Chapter Six

The only light in the cabin came from the glowing red wires of the space heater, but it was enough to reveal the tense set of Hunter's jaw and the dangerous glitter of his eyes as he peered between the drawn curtains over the front window. The helicopter had passed nearly a half hour earlier, but he was still on high alert, his ramrod posture and spare, deliberate movements convincing her all over again that he had spent at least some of his life in uniform.

"They're gone," she murmured.

His gaze cut toward her. "They could come back."

"Meanwhile, we starve to death in the dark?"

For a second, she thought he was going to bark at her like a drill sergeant and tell her to shut up and fall in line. But then he visibly relaxed, a hint of a smile conjuring up one of those rare dimples she was starting to covet. "No. I think we can manage dinner without exposing our position."

"It's not going to be an MRE or anything, is it?" she asked. She'd tried one of those military dried-food packets once, the so-called "Meals Ready to Eat." She hadn't exactly been impressed.

He slanted a curious look her way. "Why would you ask that?"

"Well, clearly you're former military."

That statement earned her a double dose of dimples. "What makes you think that?"

She ticked off the clues. "You've approached this whole thing with the planning of a field general. You carry a military-issue rucksack. And use it to carry a field kit of necessary supplies. You know your way around triage first aid. And you have the posture of a bloody soldier."

"I *was* a bloody soldier," he admitted. "A lifetime ago."

"How long a lifetime?"

He sighed as he nudged her toward the back of the house. "A little over a year."

The elusive half memory that had flitted through her mind earlier made another brief appearance before dancing beyond her reach once more. "That long, huh?"

He stopped in the middle of the kitchen and turned to look at her. "Like I said, a lifetime."

Sore spot, she thought, her gaze dropping to the leg he favored. Encased in jeans, there was nothing obviously wrong with the limb, except the limp he couldn't hide, not even here in the cabin, where the floor was level and there were no obstacles to navigate except for the occasional chair or table.

She'd never been the kind of woman who could resist poking at a sore spot. "War injury?" She nodded toward his bad leg.

The glare he shot her way would have scared a lesser woman. But Susannah had stared down her share of monsters over the span of her twenty-eight years. She didn't even flinch.

He looked away and crossed to the pantry. "Yeah."

She crowded him a little, earning another dark glare. "I should know you, shouldn't I?"

"What makes you think that?" He pulled a can of chicken and dumplings from the pantry and made a show of looking at the expiration date printed on the can in the faint orange glow of the kitchen heater.

"Well, for one thing, I keep thinking I've heard your name somewhere. Hunter's not that common a first name."

"You don't know it *is* my first name." He held the can in front of her. "Dinner?"

She nodded impatiently. "Whatever. Hunter is your first name. And you're a former soldier. And there's something—"

"Don't blow a gasket in there." He tapped her head lightly with his forefinger. "There are a couple of bowls in the cabinet over the sink, and a saucepan in the next cabinet to the right. Grab them while I get the stove going."

She fetched the stoneware bowls and a battered but clean two-quart saucepan while he lit one of the gas burners. Blue flames hissed to life, adding soft light to the warm kitchen. "Where's the can opener?" she asked, scanning the bare counter.

He pulled open a drawer and handed her a manual can opener.

"Oh, we're going old-school."

"No, old-school would be an awl and a hammer." He slanted her an amused look. "You've been away from the hills too long, Ms. Marsh."

"What makes you think I was ever in the hills?"

He turned to look at her, a hint of payback glittering in his light eyes. "Scars on your legs, the kind you get from shinning up trees and climbing rocky hills. Your nails are—were—perfectly manicured, but you can't hide the scars on your knuckles or that rope-burn scar on your palm. You've worked with those hands. Used them for more than typing." He was ticking off the clues in the same way she'd added up her conclusions about his time in the military, she noted with a mix of irritation and grudging appreciation.

"And no matter how high-priced an accent you've adopted, you still slip into a mountain twang now and then."

She closed her eyes to shut out the sight of him, wishing she could make him disappear as easily. All her hard work to completely erase her former life, and he'd seen through her in hours. "I don't know what you're talking about."

"Right." He took the can opener out of her nerveless fingers and opened the can of chicken and dumplings.

But her appetite had fled. "I think I'm too tired to eat," she said quietly, already moving out of the kitchen.

His hand closed around her wrist, pulling her to a halt. "A minute ago you were hungry enough to eat this stuff, can and all."

"Let me go."

He released her wrist. "Are you in some kind of trouble?"

Damn him, she thought. "I just spent three hours running from men with guns who want me dead. I'm being held captive in a backwoods cabin by a former soldier who won't tell me his last name. What kind of trouble could I possibly be in?"

His lips thinned to a flat line. "You should eat something. You'll sleep better."

He was right. She knew he was right. Even though her appetite was gone, her body still needed fuel, especially after her adrenaline-fed mountain hike. Relenting, she sat in one of the kitchen chairs and rested her chin on her hand, watching as he turned his attention to heating the soup.

When he was done, he poured the chicken and dumplings into the two bowls and carried them to the table where she sat, sliding one in front of her. He took a couple of spoons from a nearby drawer and handed her one. "Careful. It's hot."

She stirred the creamy soup before dipping up a spoonful and blowing to cool it. She noticed he wasn't eating any of his own soup. "Not hungry?"

He dropped his spoon back in the bowl. "No."

She threw his own words back at him. "You should eat something. You'll sleep better."

He leaned back in the chair, his chin dropping to his chest as he eyed her through a fringe of dark lashes. He looked tired. Despondent. And for the first time since he'd dragged her into the woods that night, she was beginning to believe his story.

Nobody could feign the kind of misery she saw in those green eyes.

THE RAIN ENDED OVERNIGHT, and a watery dawn seeped its way through the thicket of evergreens surrounding the cabin and slanted across Hunter's face, tugging him out of a light sleep.

He hadn't thought he'd sleep at all, given his hyperalertness when he'd finally tried to lie down and doze the night before. But after a while, even his Army training had been no match for the bone-deep weariness that had come from so much exertion after so many months of relative inactivity.

For the past couple of months, he'd been spending as much time as he could in the gym Quinn had set up in what had once been the root cellar of the old Victorian mansion that housed The Gates. The dirt floor and walls had been reinforced with concrete and softened by a springy gym floor and, in places, spongy mats where one of the agents, Sutton Calhoun, put the agents through a series of hand-to-hand combat drills to keep their skills honed to a razor edge.

Calhoun was a former Marine, another mountain boy, hailing from one of the roughest parts of the county, Smoky Ridge. The place where dreams not only went to die but to die in a spectacularly bloody and painful fashion, as Calhoun had put it one afternoon during a no-holds-barred combat drill.

"Stop feeling sorry for yourself, soldier," Calhoun had barked in his best drill-sergeant tone, throwing Hunter back to the floor and daring him to get back up.

Rubbing the ache in his shoulders, where the heavy rucksack had taken a toll, Hunter wished he could go another round with Calhoun again. His time undercover with the BRI hadn't done much for his stamina. For all their military posturing, the BRI was a militia in name only. They had some tough and very dangerous members, but those men dealt in guns, knives and bombs, not hand-to-hand combat.

He pushed himself up from the sofa and padded barefoot down the short hallway to the bathroom, listening for sounds from the nearby bedroom. The door was closed, the house silent except for the hum of electricity coursing through the walls and the sound of his bare feet on the hardwood floor. He winced a little as the bathroom door creaked while closing behind him, hoping it wouldn't disturb Susannah's sleep.

If she'd managed to get any sleep at all.

She might not be the spoiled little city girl he'd assumed, but it wasn't likely she'd ever found herself on this end of a manhunt before.

As he stepped out of the bathroom a few moments later, the bedroom door opened as well and Susannah stepped out into the hallway, turning to face him. She was dressed in the jeans and sweater he'd provided the night before, though her hair was freshly brushed and pulled back into a sleek ponytail. "I borrowed a rubber band from your dresser drawer."

"Welcome to it." He stepped out of her way, nodding toward the bathroom. "All yours."

"I used it earlier." Her eyes were winter-gray this morning, the dim light of the hallway dilating her pupils until only a fleck of hazel showed in her pale irises. "You have any eggs in the fridge? I could whip up an omelet."

He wasn't sure he trusted her sudden easy friendliness. She'd been downright combative most of the previous evening, and he doubted a night in a strange place, spent under the constant fear of discovery, would have altered her mood so completely.

So she was up to something.

But what?

"No eggs. I wasn't sure when I'd be back here, so I didn't stock any perishables."

Her dark eyebrows ticked upward, and he could tell by the flicker of her eyelids that she was processing the meaning behind his words. He could almost hear her thoughts, the complex calculations winnowed down to the basics: he planned ahead, but not far. And this bolt-hole, while well-equipped for the purpose of lying low, hadn't been his first choice.

He hadn't thought he'd need a place to hide her, if she wanted to know the truth. He'd planned to stop the plot without her ever having to know that she was on the BRI's target list.

This cabin had been a different sort of hiding place. Not from specific threats like Billy Dawson and his ragtag crew of soldier wannabes but from the world in general.

But from a life that had stopped making sense over a year ago on a dust-dry road in the Helmand Province of Afghanistan.

"So, no milk for cereal, either?"

"Sorry."

"Peanut butter and a spoon?" She punctuated the question with a toothy smile that sucker punched him straight in the gut with a lust so acute, so raw that he almost doubled over from the impact.

He nearly took a step toward her, nearly closed the narrow gap between their bodies before he had a chance to think past the pounding drumbeat of desire rattling his bones and fogging his brain.

"Yeah," he managed, turning away before he did something stupid. "There's peanut butter. And you know what? I think there may be a loaf of bread in the freezer. You could toast it." He waved her toward the kitchen while he crossed the room in three limping strides and made a show of looking through the drapes that covered the four glass panes of the back door, even though he expected to see nothing more than morning sunlight dappling the fallen leaves that littered the tiny clearing around the cabin.

"Want some?" She was making busy noises at the counter behind him.

"Sure."

"Got any jelly?"

"Check the fridge." Frost covered the leaves and grass outside, a grim reminder of how close they'd come to spending the night in a cave instead of this cozy, heated cabin. If she'd succeeded in running away from him, he couldn't have given up the hunt. Not when she was out there somewhere, barefoot and running for her life.

"Mmm, peach preserves."

He glanced over his shoulder and found Susannah watching him with sharp eyes. Her gaze softened immediately when she saw him looking, but not before he caught the feral wariness in her expression.

No, she hadn't dropped her guard a bit. But clearly she wanted him to think she had.

Why? So he'd drop his?

"This is home-canned, isn't it?" she asked brightly, giving the Mason jar lid a strong twist.

"I think so." Janet had helped stock the place, overruling his protest by assuring him that staying busy helping him get situated was a much better use of her time than sitting home worrying about what a Ridge County judge was going to decide about her fate.

Susannah looked around the kitchen, her gaze settling first on the brightly colored pot holders hanging from a hook on the wall, then at the sunny yellow curtains hanging on the windows and the door. "Girlfriend?"

His gaze snapped up to meet hers. "Sister."

"Oh." She gave a slight nod, then turned as the first pair of bread slices popped up from the toaster. "So, no girlfriend?"

"No," he answered, trying to figure out if she was really curious or if the question was another attempt to set him at ease. If so, she'd picked the wrong topic.

"Boyfriend?"

Wary or not, he couldn't stop a grin at that question. "No."

She shrugged and turned back to the counter to put two more slices of bread in the toaster. "You never know."

He stepped up behind her, noting how her body stiffened slightly as she felt his body heat wash over her. But she didn't flinch, didn't show any other sign of awareness, save for the slightest tremble of her fingers when she picked up a butter knife from the counter and dipped it into the open jar of peanut butter.

"What about you?" he asked in a low tone, bending close enough that his breath stirred the tawny hair curling in front of her ear. Definitely a natural blonde, he thought as a glint of morning sunlight stole through the narrow gap of the kitchen curtains to glimmer like gold in the pale hair closest to her scalp.

She turned around suddenly, catching him off guard. He grabbed the counter to keep from stumbling backward, and the move drew him even closer to her, so close that his hips brushed against hers.

Her lips trembled apart, but she didn't drop her gaze, staring up at him with fire in those winter-pale eyes.

"What do you really want?" she asked.

A thousand answers flooded his brain, most of them so intimate, so unsayable that for a moment, he felt as if he'd been struck dumb.

But the fog cleared almost as quickly as it had

arisen, and with an almost preternatural clarity, he knew that only one answer would suffice.

The truth.

"Absolution," he said in a voice as raw as a wound.

Chapter Seven

There was no nuance to the word. No hint that Hunter was yanking her chain or making a joke. Just a ragged-edged openness that burrowed like an ache in the center of her chest.

She fought the terrifying urge to cry and plastered on a mask of a smile. "Fresh out of absolution, sugar."

He withdrew his comforting heat from her, and the morning chill swept in to take its place. "I'd like to hike over to Bitterwood and see if I can pick up any news about your disappearance, but I don't like leaving you alone here."

"Afraid someone will find me while you're gone?"

Keeping his careful distance from her, he glanced over his shoulder and met the challenge of her gaze. "Afraid you'll bug out while I'm gone."

"I thought I wasn't a prisoner."

"You're not. That doesn't mean I want you to

leave. At least, not until I can figure out what the BRI are planning to do next."

"How're you going to do that?" Alarm fluttered in her belly. "You're not thinking you're going to just walk into the next planning meeting and pretend you had nothing to do with what happened last night, are you?"

"I'm not sure anyone saw me well enough to recognize me."

She took a couple of steps toward him before she realized what she was doing. She drew her hand back, but not before her fingertips brushed his bare forearm.

He gave her a look so scorching she felt something inside catch flame and spread until her skin felt hot and tight beneath his gaze. She made herself look away from him, but the fire didn't die. It just continued to smolder low in her belly.

She didn't trust him. Didn't particularly like him.

But apparently, she wouldn't mind wrapping herself around him and riding him like a cowboy on a wild mustang, as her grandmother used to say when she didn't know Susannah was listening.

Well, hell.

She somehow managed to find her voice and the unraveling threads of their conversation. "You can't chance it. If they did see you last night, they're as likely to shoot you dead before you open your mouth as not, right?"

"Probably," he conceded. He took care not to look at her this time, and she supposed he didn't care for all this sexual electricity zipping and zapping around them any more than she did. "I wasn't going to go stick my head in the lion's den or anything. Just thought I could try to touch base with my boss and see if he's heard anything about what happened last night."

He kept talking about his boss. What boss? Was he seriously still trying to convince her he was working some undercover angle and was actually on her side?

What kind of idiot did he think she was?

She decided to play along, for now, however. No need to antagonize the man who had her held captive, for all intents and purposes. "Do you think it's possible nobody heard the gunshots?"

He shook his head. "They weren't using sound suppressors. The noise would have carried to the hotel."

"But there were only night staff on duty. And the employee parking lot is some distance from the hotel." The more she thought about it, the more possible it seemed that the incident had passed without anyone heading down to the parking lot to see what was going on. "The woods are close, and people do go hunting out here at night, sometimes. I've heard the security guys complain about it, but they're not conservation officers, so they don't actually go out to look for the perpetrators. Most of the time they don't even report the gunfire—"

"They'll look into it when you don't show up for work this morning," he said with grim certainty.

"So, maybe I should show up for work."

His gaze snapped up to meet hers. "No."

"It would throw your merry band of domestic terrorists for a loop, wouldn't it? If I showed up for work like nothing was wrong?"

"And give them a second chance to kill you?" He closed the distance between them swiftly, all semblance of restraint gone. He caught her upper arms in his first tight grip, drawing her gaze to his. His eyes blazed with intensity, plucking her taut nerves until her whole body vibrated from the cacophony.

"You said I'm not your prisoner."

"I never said I was going to let you go back there to be killed." His grip on her arms tightened to the edge of pain. "Listen to me. I nearly didn't get to you in time. So many things could have gone very, very wrong last night and we're damn lucky they didn't. You're safe here. We've bought time to figure out what to do next. You can't throw it all away by being pigheaded and stupid."

She jerked her arms from his grasp. "Pig-headed and stupid?"

He scraped his hand through his hair, his fingers tangling in the dark mass of waves. For a second, he seemed comically surprised by the snag, confirming for Susannah her theory that he'd worn his hair military short not so very long ago.

He met her gaze again, but in a sidelong way, like a puppy who'd been caught chewing up a pair of $800 Jimmy Choos. "Strong-willed and recklessly brave?"

"Better," she relented, trying not to smile. If she smiled, she'd have to consider the notion that she liked him as well as found him smoking hot, and, well, here be monsters, matey.

"Will you stay here and stay put if I hike over the hill to Bitterwood?" he asked after a long, tense moment of silence.

"What do you plan to do there?"

"Just drop in at the diner in town, put my ear to the ground and see what shakes loose."

"What if someone recognizes you?"

"Not too many people in Bitterwood know who I am anymore," he said in a vague tone that suggested he wasn't really sure he was telling the truth.

"But they did once?"

His gaze slithered away. "Not really."

She took a deep breath and let it out slowly. "Okay. I'll stay put. Just don't be long. And don't get caught."

"I'll do my best." He nodded at the toast that had grown cold and hard while they talked. "Meanwhile, you can eat your cold toast and think of me and a plate full of Maisey Ledbetter's hot buttered biscuits and gravy."

"You're such a tool." She picked up one of the pieces of toast and threw it at him as he ducked out of the kitchen, heading for the front of the house.

The second pair of bread slices popped up out of the toaster, and she snagged them before they could cool down, telling herself as she munched the peanut butter-and-jelly-slathered toast that she didn't envy Hunter's oh-so-fattening biscuit-and-gravy breakfast one little bit.

Then she cleaned up quickly, mentally calculated how long she thought Hunter might be gone on his morning trip to Bitterwood, and got to work.

If she was right, he'd be gone no less than an hour, no more than two and a half. He'd taken his rucksack with him, she found as she looked around the front room, checking the small closet close to the fireplace as well as the big footlocker chest that doubled as a coffee table.

The closet was empty. The footlocker, on the

other hand, was full. On top of the pile were a couple of spare pillows and a thermal blanket he'd probably used last night to ward off the chill while he slept on the sofa.

Below that, however, she hit pay dirt.

The first item she encountered was a set of dog tags. Bragg, Hunter M. His blood type—A positive—and a nine-digit Social Security number, no spaces or dashes. U.S. Army. Sounded right.

An Army soldier named Hunter Bragg. Why did that seem so familiar?

When the memory hit, it hit hard, spreading a hard chill through her limbs. She sank to the sofa in front of the open footlocker, clutching the dog tags so tightly they dug into her palms.

He'd been kidnapped by elements of the BRI a little over a year ago, taken captive as leverage against his sister. They'd used Hunter to blackmail the woman into drugging her boss, a prosecutor, so that the BRI could kidnap a little boy the prosecutor had been keeping under his protection.

The pictures in the newspaper had been gut-wrenching—the wounded warrior, home after a harrowing near-death experience overseas, now brutalized by homegrown thugs who'd left him battered beyond recognition. The photo of his bloodied, swollen face had won regional photography awards, if she remembered correctly, but it hadn't been the injuries that had caught the judges' imaginations.

It had been the expression on Hunter Bragg's face that had elevated the snapshot to journalistic art. The photo had shown the expected pain and rage in the man's face, of course, but beneath those obvious emotions had roiled a vortex of humiliation and disillusion. So much raw human suffering captured in the blink of a camera lens—Susannah hadn't been able to look at the photo for long before she averted her eyes.

A creak on the wooden porch outside gave her no time to react, but as the front door opened, she reached into the footlocker and grabbed the scabbard that lay half-hidden beneath an olive-drab canteen. In a heartbeat, she'd closed her hand around the knife handle and swept it neatly from the scabbard. Light pouring through the opening door glittered on the shiny steel edge, bouncing a splash of light across Hunter's scowling face as he slammed the door behind him.

"What the hell are you doing?"

With shaking hands, she eased the knife back into the scabbard and dropped it atop the spare blanket. "Snooping," she admitted.

His expression hardening, he crossed to where she sat and closed the footlocker firmly. "There are people out in the woods not too far from here. Looks like they're gathering for a search party."

"You're Hunter Bragg."

He didn't look at her, but in his darkened expression, she saw a hint of that same humiliation and disillusion that had so struck her in his photo. "There's a place to hide in the cellar. In case anyone stumbles on this place and wants a look around."

"Did you infiltrate the BRI for revenge?"

His eyes closed briefly, then opened slowly. He finally looked up, meeting her gaze. "Revenge rarely works the way you think it will. I prefer to think of what I'm doing as seeking justice."

She nodded, understanding the distinction even though she wasn't really sure there was much difference between a thirst for revenge and the willing assumption of dangerous risk Hunter was taking with the BRI.

"How did you ever talk them into letting you join? They took you hostage—"

"That's how," he answered. "I went to Billy Dawson and told him they could have saved themselves the trouble if they'd just come to me first. I would have gladly contributed my services to the group if they'd just let me know what they were up to."

"And they believed you?"

"People believe what they want to. I convinced them I could be an asset. The group has been reeling ever since their leader got captured.

They're looking for a resurgence. I made them see I could be a vital part of it."

"As a disgruntled ex-soldier?"

"Why not? They like to fashion themselves as patriots." He shrugged. "I don't think those searchers out there will find this place right away. They'll probably stick to the beaten path, at least at first, and there's supposed to be rain this afternoon, which will probably cut the search short."

"But they'll be back."

"They will," he agreed. "Somebody probably found your car in the lot at the hotel. There may have been bullet holes."

"They'll think someone took me and dragged me into the woods." She couldn't quite stop a wry smile from quirking her lips, since that was pretty much what had happened.

"I know." He dropped onto the sofa beside her, resting his elbows on his knees. His head dipped until his chin almost reached his chest. "We need a plan."

"You don't have one?" she asked, alarmed. As crazy as the past several hours of her life had been, she'd assumed that Hunter had taken her here to this cabin for some purpose. But he was apparently no more certain as to what to do next than she was. "Did you think you'd just snatch me from the parking lot and wing it?"

He turned his head, slanting a dark look her

way. "My goal was to get you out of there without any bullet holes in you. Get you somewhere we could hunker down for a little while and figure out the next part."

"So this is where it's time to figure out the next part?" She clamped down firmly on the urge to have a rip-roaring panic attack, clenching her hands together so tightly in her lap that her fingers began to tingle.

"I can't reach my boss."

That's it. She was over this cryptic garbage. "And who, pray tell, is your boss?"

"The guy who runs that new private investigations agency over in Purgatory. Alexander Quinn." He eyed her, as if he thought she might know the man he was talking about.

But the name meant nothing to her. "Is that unusual? Not being able to reach him?"

"He told me if I ever tried to contact him and couldn't reach him, I had to assume our line of communication had been compromised."

"What does that mean?"

He worried his lower lip with his teeth for a minute, his brow furrowed with thought. "I think we have to assume we're on our own here, at least until Quinn finds a way to contact me."

"And what if he doesn't?"

"Then I have to find some way to get us to Purgatory without being caught. If I can get you to

The Gates, we can figure out a plan of attack with a hell of a lot more resources than I have here."

"What about the law-enforcement conference?" she asked, thinking about the two hundred–plus men and women who were supposed to be meeting at the hotel's conference center wing in just about forty-eight hours. Including her cousin. "Getting me out of there, even if I'm alive, served their purposes, didn't it? Someone will have to take my place."

"Who would that be?" he asked.

"I guess Marcus."

"Marcus Lemonde."

She looked up at him. "You already knew the answer to that question before you asked it, didn't you?"

"Call it an educated guess. I knew they were trying to remove you in order to put someone of their own inside the plans for conference security. Apparently they couldn't get anyone inside security itself, so—"

"So they focused on the Events and Conferences office." And Marcus Lemonde had been working with her for a little over a month—had he been in the Blue Ridge Infantry's pocket the whole time? Or had they offered him enough money to make treachery worthwhile?

"I ran into Lemonde in the hall outside the meeting rooms, not long after you went in there for your meeting with security. I'd seen him around the hotel, but he'd never spoken to me before then."

"What did he say?"

"That they'd moved up their plans. He didn't like that I was up there on the same floor as you. I guess he thought it might make you suspicious, and since they'd decided to make their move last night—"

"I can't believe Marcus of all people—" She wasn't naive; life had taught her some pretty pointed lessons about just how treacherous people could be, even people who seemed as if they could be trusted.

But Marcus Lemonde seemed wholly innocuous, incapable of posing a threat. If he'd met her in that parking lot one on one, even armed, she would have bet she'd have a better-than-even chance of coming out the winner.

"Looks can be deceiving," Hunter said quietly.

She glanced his way, taking in the shaggy, tangled hair, the day's growth of dark beard, the sharp green eyes, and realized that less than twenty-four hours earlier, she'd actually felt pity for him, with his hangdog demeanor and limping gait.

"They can," she agreed. "And now he's going to be completely on the inside of the security plans for the conference."

"Looks that way."

She shook her head, frustration and anger swelling like a runaway tide in the center of her chest. "No way. No way in hell am I letting that slimy little turncoat weasel screw up my conference."

Pushing to her feet, she started toward the front door of the cabin.

He caught her at the door, his grip as strong as steel. She snapped her gaze up to meet his as his grasp tightened enough to hurt. "Get your hands off me."

He loosened his hold but didn't let go completely. "You can't just barge back into the hotel, Susannah. The people who want you out of the way haven't gone away."

"I show up, we thwart the plan. We tell the world what's going on and not even the BRI mole on the Barrowville police force can keep us from stopping the attack on the conference."

As she started to pull away from his grasp, he tightened his grip again. "You can't just rush out there. If that helicopter we heard is the good guys, the bad guys will damn well be out there trying to get to you first. We're a good three miles from anything that resembles civilization."

"Are you suggesting I save myself at the risk of hundreds of cops who have no idea their conference is about to be blown to smithereens or whatever the hell it is your BRI idiots are planning?" she snapped, trying to jerk her arm away from his tight hold.

He cupped her chin with his free hand, forcing her to look at him. His green eyes glittered with a curious mix of determination and fear. "I'm suggesting you stop for a minute and think about your next move. If you go out there now, without a plan or any idea of what you're up against, all you'll be doing is making damn sure that the BRI gets rid of you as planned. And that's not going to help anyone at that conference, is it?"

He was right. She knew he was right, and maybe if the Tri-State Law Enforcement Society gathering was any other conference, attended by any random set of cops, she wouldn't have led with her heart instead of her head.

But it wasn't just any conference. And at least one of the cops who'd be there in forty-eight hours wasn't random at all.

McKenna Rigsby and her parents had taken Susannah under their protection after everything had gone wrong in Boneyard Ridge, hiding her from the Bradburys until she was able to change her name, her appearance and almost everything about her that would tie her to the tow-headed tomboy she'd been when she fled the mountains.

"My cousin is one of the cops who'll be at the

conference," she said. "I owe her more than I could ever explain."

The sharp look of sympathy in his evergreen eyes stung. She looked down at his hand on her arm, watched his fingers loosen and fall away.

"Okay," he said after a stretch of silence filled only by the thud of her pulse in her ears. "We'll figure out a way to stop this thing. But we have to have a plan. Agreed?"

She made herself open her eyes, taking in the determined set of his square jaw and the fire of conviction in his gaze. The heat of that fire swept over her, driving away the morning chill and sparking delicious blazes low in her belly.

Joining forces with a man like Hunter Bragg might be the most dangerous thing she'd ever done. And she'd done some very dangerous things in her life.

But she took a deep breath, sketched a quick nod and said, "Agreed."

Chapter Eight

"Wow. You got all of this put together in the short time you worked at the hotel?"

Hunter looked up from the spread of papers and maps on the kitchen table and found Susannah looking at him through narrowed eyes, as if she was already regretting her decision to play this thing his way. But somewhere in the glittering gray depth of those hazel-tipped eyes, he also saw a hint of grudging admiration that sent an alarming amount of pleasure zinging along his nerve endings.

Once her initial agitation had settled down to a simmer, she'd taken a quick shower and changed into a fresh pair of jeans and another one of the sweaters he'd purchased in Barrowville, this time a jewel green, snug-fitting V-neck that hugged her curves like a Ferrari on a mountain switchback and brought out hints of misty green in her soft gray eyes.

Everything about her was softer today, as if

she'd shrugged off a coat of armor when she'd tossed the bedraggled remains of her business suit into the trash can in the bedroom. Her hair, free of whatever products she used to achieve that perfect, unshakable updo she wore when she was working, hung in soft, still-damp waves around her face and shoulders. Without makeup, she was a different sort of beautiful than he was used to, all dewy pink skin and a hint of tiny freckles across the bridge of her straight nose. She'd shed nearly a decade in the process, looking not much older than some of the fresh-faced baby recruits he'd known in the Army.

"It was a little longer than that," he answered her question, dragging his gaze from her with way too much reluctance. Clearly, he should have given some thought to the logistics of holing up in a cabin with a beautiful woman. Between combat, his injuries and his sister's legal troubles, his sexual needs hadn't exactly been a priority.

As soon as he could get through this mission, he would take time to think about what came next, including his sex life. But he couldn't let himself be derailed by lust when so much was on the line.

Besides, so what if Susannah Marsh had a soft

side? It didn't make her any less trouble, and the last thing he needed was more trouble.

"How long has— What's your agency? The Gates?"

He nodded.

"How long has The Gates been looking into the Blue Ridge Infantry?"

"For a while, though not in conjunction with the conference." The conference connection information had dropped into their laps by way of a confidential informant Quinn worked with. Hunter didn't know who the C.I. was, but Quinn thought his source was reliable, and Hunter supposed he would know. "They were part of a multistate crime organization that several of the local law enforcement agencies have been trying to roll up and put away for a couple of years now."

"The last I heard, they'd accomplished that goal. Something about a bunch of files that was practically a road map of the entire organization?" She sent him a sidelong look, and the wariness he saw in those sharp eyes made him wonder if she was just humoring him with her cooperation, looking for a chance to make her break. "I've never read or heard anything different."

"They're like cockroaches. No matter how many you step on, there are always more."

"Didn't your boss inform the cops that there might be a problem with the conference?"

"He did. Nothing came of it. That's how we became pretty sure that there's someone in the Barrowville PD. who's on the take. Or hell, maybe even a true believer."

"What, exactly, would constitute a true believer in the BRI?" She sounded genuinely curious. "You said earlier they think of themselves as patriots."

"They'd like to believe that. Mostly, though, their idea of patriotism is a loathing for authority, I guess." At least, that was how he'd played it when he'd wormed his way into the local cell after Quinn had given him the name of someone The Gates suspected might be a BRI member. "All I had to do was make some noise about how the Pentagon had screwed me over after my injury, and now the government was railroading my sister, and it didn't take long for someone to buy my load of garbage."

"You must have sold it well."

He shrugged. "Wasn't that hard. There have been days when I half believed it myself. There's a fine line between authority and despotism. Gets crossed a little too often for my taste, you know?"

She nodded. "I do, actually. And it's not always the government."

"Oh, I know. I've seen how Billy Dawson runs

the local BRI cell. Tin-pot dictators have nothing on him."

"Nobody at the Barrowville PD even checked on what you were saying about the conference?" A hint of her previous skepticism seeped into her question.

"Police forces in this neck of the woods have a serious corruption problem. But even if they didn't, there's the issue of how these local cops see The Gates."

"As interlopers?"

"Something like that. See, Quinn has this thing about hiring people who maybe don't have the best of track records." He couldn't keep the wry tone from his voice.

"Does that include you?"

"Maybe. I was a wild kid, and if you were to go by the way I've been behaving over the past year or so, you wouldn't think I'd changed that much." He'd gotten into his share of bar fights since returning home from overseas. He couldn't even blame it on booze, since he'd been stone-cold sober every time. Drinking hadn't done a thing to stem the pain and anger.

Of course, the fights hadn't done much to make him feel better, either. He'd supposed, at the time, that pure luck had brought Alexander Quinn into Smoky Joe's Saloon a few months ago in time to stop a brewing fight and hand his business card to Hunter with an offer of a job interview.

Now that he'd worked with Quinn for a while, he realized that the man had probably gone to the bar with the express purpose of recruiting him for The Gates. Quinn didn't do anything without a plan.

He just wished he knew what Quinn's plan was at the moment, because sitting around and waiting wasn't his style. But he'd seen too many missions go belly-up when someone down the chain of command decided to change things on the fly without having all the information.

"What are you thinking?" Susannah asked.

Glancing up, he saw her studying him with eyes too sharp for his liking. The woman was turning out to be nothing like what he'd thought she'd be. He'd figured her for smart, but he hadn't banked on her being so observant and insightful that he'd feel like a bug she'd pinned under a microscope for further study.

"What makes you think I'm thinking anything?"

She reached up suddenly, her fingertips brushing his forehead. "This little line. It appears when you're trying to figure things out."

He tried to relax his face as she dropped her fingers away, but the feel of her cool touch lingered on his brow. "And you know this because we're such old, close friends."

"I know this because I pay attention." She reached out again, this time touching the muscle directly behind his collarbone. "Your trapezius muscle tenses up when you're worried."

"Doesn't everyone's?" He knew a frontal attack when he saw one. Every instinct told him she was trying to unnerve him with her touch. Maybe that was her way of regaining some sense of control over her life.

Problem was, it was working. Even the slightest flutter of her fingertips against his skin had sent heat rushing south to his groin. If she ever put her mind to seducing him...

She dropped her hand away from his shoulder, and it took an effort not to groan in response. Her gaze sharpened as it met his. "I know a lot about that hotel, Hunter. I know how things work, where things are, who does what. I can help you if you'll just let me in on what you're planning."

He wasn't much for trusting other people under the best of circumstances, and his current situation certainly didn't qualify for best of anything. But she had proved to be a lot tougher—and tougher-minded—than he'd expected. And it wasn't like Quinn was going out of his way to get in touch.

He needed an ally. Inaction wasn't in his

nature, either, and if he didn't figure out something to do soon, something that might actually make the situation better rather than worse, he was going to go crazy.

"Okay," he said, releasing the word in a resigned sigh. "I'll tell you what I'm thinking. But I don't know if you're going to like it."

HE WAS RIGHT. She didn't like it. Not one bit. "I'm not going to hole up here in this cabin while you sneak back into the hotel."

"You asked to hear my plan. That's it." His chin jutting stubbornly toward her, he folded his arms across his chest, stretching his shirt across his broad shoulders and powerful chest, a visual reminder that, for all her bluster, she would be no match against this man in a fair fight.

Of course, she'd never had any compunction about fighting dirty if necessary.

"Are you going to lock me in here against my will? Because that would add a lovely little felony to your record."

He sighed again, a long, gusty one that showed her just what he thought of her refusal to play by his rules. "You're free to go. And be grabbed by people who want you dead before you ever get close to the edge of these woods."

She wasn't so sure about that. Now that she had shoes, appropriate clothing and access to supplies, she might be better at sneaking out of these woods than he thought. Sure, this wasn't Boneyard Ridge, but her little hometown wasn't that much farther up the Appalachian chain, only a few miles down the highway that connected several small mountain towns in the Smokies.

Close enough to give her a fighting chance at finding her way around. She knew what the terrain was like. She knew how to find her direction using the position of the sun at this time of year in this part of Tennessee.

"If I leave here without you, you really are going to make a run for it, aren't you?"

She didn't answer, but she could tell he saw through her silence. That furrow came back to his brow, and his trapezius muscle looked as hard as a rock.

He turned away abruptly. "Would you stop looking at my shoulders?"

She couldn't stop a soft huff of laughter. "Why are you fighting this so hard? You one of those guys who thinks a woman can't do anything without a man showing her the way?"

He turned so swiftly he almost lost his balance, and she saw a grimace of pain flit across his features as the leg he favored twisted. Putting his weight on the other leg, he swung the injured one straight and resettled his weight on both limbs. "You don't know me. Don't presume to know what I think about anything."

"I can only go by your behavior."

"And I can only go by yours."

Her smile faded. "What the hell is that supposed to mean?"

He reached out and caught her hand, his gaze narrowing a little as he took in the clipped fingernails. "What would you do if you weren't here? You'd go get a manicure." He dropped her hand, but the tingle of his touch seemed to linger. "You had to run barefoot through the woods because you wear four-inch heels to work instead of comfortable shoes."

"Heels can be comfortable," she protested, annoyed that he was practically echoing the internal argument she had with herself nearly every day. She could well imagine exactly what kind of woman he thought she was because it was the facade she'd fought hard to present to the world, the armor she wore against discovery.

"Then why do you hide comfortable shoes in your desk?"

"You went through my desk?" Her mind swept quickly through her desk drawers, wondering what else he might have discovered. She tended to keep her personal life out of the office, but there was her chocolate stash—

"It was part of my job," he said, surprising her by looking a little embarrassed.

"Then I'm sure you know appearances can be deceiving."

"Why do you dye your hair brown? And wear brown contacts?"

"Ever heard any dumb-blonde jokes?"

His eyes narrowed. "Nobody would mistake you for a dumb anything."

"Thanks. I think."

He took a couple of slow, deliberate steps toward her. "I know when someone's hiding something. And you, darlin', are hiding a whole lot of something. Which makes me very nervous."

"I'm not the one who took a job at the hotel under false pretenses." Which was a lie, of course, but he didn't know it was.

He couldn't know, could he?

"Are you connected to the BRI?" His voice was warm velvet, but she could sense the steel beneath.

She almost wilted with relief. He didn't know. He wasn't even close. "Are you crazy? I thought you said the BRI was trying to kill me."

"They are. But why?"

"To put Marcus Lemonde in charge of the conference. Isn't that what you told me?"

"I did," he admitted, his eyes slightly narrowed. "But you know, you have a few tells of your own." He pushed her hair back from her forehead, touching one rough fingertip to the skin beneath her left eye. "Your eye twitches right here when you feel threatened. I noticed it last night in the cave. Twitching away." His fingertip lingered for a moment, then traced a slow, shiver-inducing trail over the curve of her cheek and down to the side of her neck. "What are you afraid of now? You're safe here, aren't you?"

"Am I?" She hated the weakness of her voice, the sudden hammering of her pulse beneath his touch.

"As safe as you want to be." His gaze dipped to her mouth, and fire arced its way through her belly. The heat of his body, so close to hers, was as powerful as a magnet, tugging her toward him before she realized what she was doing.

His gaze flicked up to meet hers, his eyes dark and deep. He wanted her. She could almost feel the desire coming off him in waves, enveloping her in a maelstrom of heat.

Slowly, as if giving her time to react, he slid his hand around the back of her neck and tugged her even closer, his breath warm against her lips. "How safe do you want to be?"

Safer than this, she thought, taking a step that she meant to propel herself backward. But somehow, she ended up even closer to him, close enough that her hips brushed against his, eliciting a quick gasp of breath between his parted lips.

A faint vibration ran through her where their bodies met. She didn't realize until Hunter growled a soft profanity and took a step away that what she was feeling was his phone buzzing quietly in the pocket of his jeans. "This is Quinn. I have to take this."

She took advantage of the timely pause to expand the distance between them, crossing to one of the cabin windows and gazing out at the sun-dappled side yard. The small clearing where the cabin sat was barely large enough to contain the cabin. What lawn existed was a narrow, browning patch of halfhearted grass swallowed within a few yards by the encroaching woods.

This place was well-hidden, she thought. People who lived within easy walking distance might go a lifetime without realizing this cabin and its enigmatic owner existed at all.

By design, she thought, sparing a glance toward Hunter. He stood near the fireplace heater, his head bent as he listened to the man named Quinn.

"I understand," he said finally, slanting a quick look at Susannah. She turned her head back to the window before their gazes connected. "I'll see if I can make that happen."

She waited to see if the conversation continued, but after several seconds, she realized he'd already hung up the phone. She angled another look his way.

He was still standing by the hearth, one arm propped up on the mantel. His gaze seemed fixed on the stone floor of the hearth, his expression grim.

"What does he want to do?" she asked.

His gaze flicked up and locked with hers. "He wants me to find a way back into the hotel. We're no closer to knowing what they were planning than we were last night when everything went down. And we've lost almost a day's worth of investigation."

Her mind rebelled at the thought. The place would be swarming with cops, and they wouldn't stand still and let him explain why he hadn't shown up to work the morning after the hotel's director of events and conferences had gone missing. "How're you supposed to do that without getting caught?"

One dark eyebrow ticked upward. "Is that concern I hear, Ms. Marsh?"

Annoyed by his flippant tone, she pressed her lips shut and didn't answer.

His shoulders rose and fell on a sigh. "I'll figure something out. I have the map of the hotel layout—"

"Does the map show the secret entrance in the executive parking deck?" she asked.

His eyes darkened. "No, it doesn't. There's a secret entrance?"

"I don't know how secret it is, really—I'm sure that the people who run hotel operations know it's there. But it must be fairly secret, because they don't cover it with security and it's never locked."

"And you know this how?"

"I'm an executive."

"But you park all the way down in the employee parking lot."

"So?"

"And you made a note in your phone about joining a gym." He turned to look at her, his gaze sweeping over her in a quick but thorough assessment. "It's the chocolate stash, right? Gained a pound or two, so you're parking in the lower forty so you have to get some extra exercise?"

"You were right. You're definitely not a gentleman."

"I did warn you." He pushed away from the fireplace and crossed to where she stood by the window, his movements slow and deliberate, as if giving her the chance to flee if she wanted to. But she couldn't seem to move.

The heat of him poured over her again, and she felt the strangest sense of relief, as if she'd been waiting for him to return. He lifted one hand and tucked a strand of hair behind her ear. "And in case it means anything, there's not one damn thing wrong with your body." His lips quirked with a crooked smile. "Chocolate looks good on you."

"Don't jump the gun there, hotshot." She flashed him a cheeky grin, even though her insides were quivering. "It's a little early in our acquaintance for you to be picturing me in chocolate."

The phone he still held in his left hand buzzed again. He closed his eyes, taking a swift breath through his nose. "Really?" he muttered to the phone, frustration keen in his voice.

She turned back to the window, waiting for him to drift away again. But his heat remained, cocooning her as his gravelly voice rumbled close to her ear. "What now?"

She heard the faint, tinny sound of a voice in response, though she couldn't make out any words. But there was no mistaking the crackle of tension that ripped through the room a second before Hunter's arm wrapped around her shoulders and dragged her backward, away from the window.

"What?" she managed, before he pressed his palm against her mouth, silencing her.

Then she heard the footsteps. Heavy thuds

on the wooden porch outside, moving closer. A pause as thick as molasses in December, then a nerve-shattering trio of raps on the door.

"Anybody home?" The voice was low, drawling. Unfamiliar.

"Not a word," Hunter whispered in her ear.

Chapter Nine

It was impossible to determine friendlies from enemies from the cockpit of an ordinary commercial helicopter gliding over a thicket of evergreens and leaf-shedding hardwoods at a hundred miles an hour, but Alexander Quinn had decided that anybody approaching the well-hidden cabin where his newest operative had holed up should be considered a potential threat. So when he'd spotted the two men heading toward the cabin during the last pass-by, he called Hunter Bragg's secondary burner phone and gave him a heads-up.

He hadn't bothered with the first phone he'd given Bragg shortly before the man went undercover. He'd already established the line of contact between that phone and his own had most likely been compromised.

But by whom? It infuriated Quinn to think that someone might have gotten past his byzantine security system, even though people had been raising eyebrows at his choices of operatives ever since the doors to The Gates first opened. The son of a con artist had been one of his first hires. An actual con artist had followed. A couple of slightly disgraced FBI agents—disgraced not by dishonor, of course, but by putting honor above the bureau—had joined the motley crew. A former CIA double agent who'd spent time on the FBI's most-wanted list for terrorism in South America. An ex-Marine living under suspicion of an eighteen-year-old murder. A former Diplomatic Security Service agent with a record of fighting the system.

All good agents for The Gates, or so he'd thought.

Had he been wrong?

He heard the sound of three loud raps, then a whisper, barely audible, on the other end of the chopper's satellite phone. "Not a word," Bragg whispered, apparently to the woman.

He heard the faint rustle of movement, the snick of a door opening and closing. Then the line went dead.

He put the satellite phone back in its holder and looked at the other passenger in the chopper. The man across from him raised an eyebrow but didn't bother speaking. The roar of the rotors made dialogue impossible without using headsets, and neither of them was inclined to risk putting anything into the ether that might be intercepted. It wasn't likely the strutting imposters of the so-called Blue Ridge Infantry had the equipment to snag in-air chatter, but Quinn wasn't sure they were working alone.

Someone had changed the plan for Susannah Marsh's murder in the middle of the game, and only a chance meeting with another BRI operative, one neither Quinn nor Bragg had known was in place at the hotel, had allowed Quinn's agent to get the woman to safety in time.

They had to be very careful how they proceeded from here on. He'd keep contact to a minimum and trust Bragg to run the operation on the ground.

The Army vet didn't realize it, but Quinn's decision to tap him as an operative for The Gates hadn't been a fluke or even an act of pity, as Quinn suspected Bragg believed. Before the IED explosion that had nearly taken Bragg's life and ended his Army career, Bragg had been an exceptional warrior, valued by his men and his superiors alike for his quick mind and fearless leadership.

Quinn believed a man's character didn't change just because he'd taken a body blow in combat. Bragg might have been having trouble getting back on his feet after the injury, but the warrior was still there, aching to get out and do what he'd been trained to do.

Quinn could use that warrior in the mission he'd undertaken. He sure as hell hadn't been willing to let Hunter Bragg waste away in a quagmire of guilt and anger without giving him a chance to salvage that part of himself that still had much to offer the world.

Now he'd just have to trust that he hadn't overestimated the man's ability to swim instead of sink.

THE CELLAR BENEATH the cabin was small, taking up only half the length of the house, but beyond the stone walls of the basement room was a narrow tunnel carved in the rocky soil and reinforced with concrete. There was an outside exit, if they were forced to use it, well-hidden fifteen yards past the tree line east of the cabin. He hoped they wouldn't have to use it, but if the person or persons still knocking on the cabin door decided to come in and take a look around, they'd have to make a run for it.

They hadn't turned on any lights that morning, the daylight filtering through the windows the only illumination, but the heaters had run all night. Even though he'd flipped the switch on the heater in the front room, nobody who entered the front room would be fooled that the cabin was uninhabited.

At least there was a dead bolt on the front door.

If their unexpected visitor was a civilian searcher, the locked door might be enough to send him on his way. An unlocked door might have been better, and a cold parlor, but that option wasn't available.

He'd hoped the secluded cabin would be far enough from the hotel or any well-used hiking trail to be a reasonable hiding place.

He'd underestimated the reach of the Ridge County Sheriff's Department.

"Who do you think it is?" Susannah's voice was a faint whisper in the darkened cellar. There was no light here in the cellar at all, though he'd grabbed a flashlight from the kitchen on his way downstairs.

"Probably someone from the search party for you."

"I thought we were far enough from the hotel that they wouldn't come out here."

"So did I. We were apparently wrong."

Her hand closed around his wrist, cool and remarkably steady, given the way she'd trembled beneath his touch earlier as he led her downstairs. "What if it's not someone from the search party?"

"I'm not sure it matters to us either way. We can't risk being found."

"Not even by the cops?"

"Do you know which cops you can trust and which ones will sell you out in a heartbeat?"

She was silent for a long moment. "No."

There was an odd tone to her voice that piqued his curiosity, but he shoved his interest to the back of his mind to consider later. Right now, he had to figure out what to do if he heard someone enter the cabin above.

The floorboards creaked quite audibly when someone was in the cabin overhead. He'd learned that fact when Janet had helped him move his stuff into the place when he first returned from Afghanistan and decided to make it his getaway. It wasn't officially in his name; Janet still held the deed. It wouldn't be the first place Billy Dawson looked for him, since he'd let Billy think he was estranged from Janet, that he'd hated her job with the county prosecutor's office and she'd hated his political views. He'd hoped it would be enough to protect his sister from trouble if his undercover work went belly-up.

God, he wished he could talk to her right now, let her know everything would be okay.

"Either way, whether they come in or not, we can't stay here after this," he murmured. "You realize that, don't you?"

She remained silent, though her fingers tightened around his wrist.

"I know you don't trust me. But I'm asking you

to take a chance here. Even if the people knocking at the door go away, we can't risk staying here now that someone knows this place exists. They may go find the cops, get someone who can break in and take a look around. Sooner or later, they'll connect this cabin to me and then they're going to turn it upside down."

"Because you're their primary suspect in my abduction."

He nodded. "I go missing from the hotel the same day you go missing? Hell, yeah, they're going to think the worst."

"Would they be wrong?"

"Technically, I guess not."

They fell silent, the only sound in the small cellar the whisper of their breathing. Overhead, the cabin remained eerily quiet.

"Do you think they went away?" Her whisper broke the stillness a few moments later, plucking his nerves.

"I don't know," he admitted softly. "I need to go up there and check. Can I trust you to stay put?"

"Nowhere to go but up there with you."

He hadn't told her about the outside exit, he realized. He probably should tell her now, but he wasn't sure he could trust her not to make a run for it. She was strong-willed and hardheaded, traits he ordinarily liked in a woman—unless those traits led her to make risky choices.

But leaving her stuck down here, defenseless, if he met with trouble upstairs would be putting her in harm's way. She was a smart woman, and more resourceful in a crisis than he'd thought. She had a right to make her own decisions, either way.

"There's a door hidden behind that old broken armoire in the corner. When you open the armoire, you'll see it's empty and all the shelves have been removed. Just step into it. There's a pressure switch in the bottom that opens the door to a tunnel that leads to a door outside." He put the flashlight in her hand. "If I'm not back in five minutes, you go. It leads to an escape hatch in the woods."

She was silent for a long moment before her fingers closed over the flashlight, brushing his. "Who are you?"

"The better question might be, who was my grandfather?" he murmured. "He worked at the Oak Ridge National Laboratory during the height of the Cold War."

"A scientist?"

"A maintenance man, but he saw and heard enough to be paranoid about nuclear war, so he did what he could, in his limited way, to build himself a shelter in case the Soviets dropped the big one." He couldn't hold back a wry smile, even though she couldn't see it in the dark. "His understanding of nuclear fallout was clearly limited, but you can't fault him for his will to survive."

"Okay. Five minutes."

As he started toward the stairs to the main floor, she grabbed his arm, her fingers tight. He stopped, turning back toward her, and their bodies collided with a light thump, the softness and the steel of her pressing intimately against him. He found it suddenly impossible to breathe.

"Be careful," she whispered, her fingers convulsing briefly around his arm before she let him go and backed away, robbing him of her soft heat.

Sucking air into his burning lungs, he felt his way to the stairs and climbed as silently as he could. The door creaked faintly as he eased it back open, the sound skating down his back on a razor's edge of alarm. Staying very still, he listened.

The knocking sounds had subsided a few minutes earlier. There were no sounds of occupation, save for his own carefully shallow respirations. No creak of the wooden floor. No rustle of clothing. Everything was utterly quiet.

Edging through the narrow opening of the doorway, he eased down the short corridor to the front room. It was empty. His footsteps sounded like thunder as he crossed quickly to the front window and peered through the narrow gap in the curtains with one eye.

Two men walked away from the cabin slowly, with no attempt at stealth or any show of distress or alarm. One of the men was speaking into a phone. Calling in a report of their attempt to enter the cabin to look for the missing woman?

They'd be back. There was no way the county sheriff's department would leave a cabin in the woods unexamined as long as Susannah Marsh was missing.

They'd bought some time, but not much.

He crossed back to the cellar door and called softly. "They're gone. You can come back up."

For a long, tense moment, there was no sound from below. Then he heard her footsteps on the wood stairs and his heart started beating again.

"Did you see them?" she asked as she emerged from the stairwell.

"Just their backs. Looks like a couple of search-and-rescue volunteers. One of them was on the phone."

"Reporting the existence of the cabin?"

He nodded grimly. "I'm sorry. I was hoping we'd have a little more time here."

She gave him a considering look before her expression softened and she gave a slight shrug of her shoulders. "What good is it doing us to hole up here, anyway? It's not going to stop whatever your buddies have planned for the conference."

"Yeah. And they're not my buddies."

She gave him another one of her laser-sharp looks. He could almost feel the heat of her scrutiny, as if she'd somehow burrowed her way inside his brain and started sifting around to see what was there. He was both intrigued and unnerved, and it took most of his self-control not to look away.

"Remember I was telling you that I had access to the executive parking deck at the hotel?" she said just before his control snapped.

He nodded. "Yeah, you didn't finish your thought earlier." A flood of heat poured through him as he remembered why.

Her eyes darkened. "Well, what I was going to tell you is that since the door has no security system, I can get us into the hotel without anyone knowing about it."

"But how are we going to get into the executive parking deck without a vehicle that has an access sticker or whatever it is that lets you in?"

"That's the thing," she said with a grin so cheeky and appealing he almost kissed her right then and there. "Half the battle of any security system is putting up a stern front. But it's mostly show. There are all kinds of holes in the security system at the hotel. Not for the guest rooms of course—management takes guest security and privacy really seriously. And they're careful about cash handling and all that. But for getting in and out of the place? Really not that hard."

He gave her a considering look of his own. "You sound like a thief."

Her eyes narrowed slightly. "Not me. I'm honest as the day is long."

SUSANNAH WASN'T LYING. She wasn't a thief. But her daddy could have written a book on the topic, and he'd taught her just about everything he knew about parting people from their hard-earned cash.

Her grandmother had plucked her out of that situation fast enough, once she realized her daughter had run off and left Susannah and her brother, Jimmy, with their shiftless daddy. Jimmy had run away from their grandmother's place and gone back home to be his father's little sticky-handed apprentice, but Susannah had fought to stay with her grandmother.

Her grandmother hadn't been soft, sweet or maternal, which probably explained Susannah's own mother's desperate need for love and attention. But her grandmother had loved Susannah in her own way, in a pragmatic and fierce way. And that kind of love was better than the selfish claptrap her father tossed around and called affection.

Susannah supposed she was very much like her grandmother where the heart was concerned. Feelings were no substitute for good sense. Feelings would steer you wrong every time. Good sense always carried the day.

"What aren't you telling me?" Hunter asked softly.

She ignored his question. "We've got to get out of here fast, right?"

"Pretty fast. They might not get back here in the next couple of hours, but they'll be back to take a look around."

"So let's not waste any more time talking. Do you have an extra backpack around here for me? That way we could take double the supplies."

"You sure you want extra weight? Where I'm taking you is a two-mile hike up the mountain."

She stifled a groan at the thought. Working a desk job had taken a toll on her endurance, but she was young and mostly fit. Her feet would probably hurt like hell, but there was nothing structurally wrong with her feet, and pain alone wouldn't kill her.

She lifted her chin and met his gaze. "I can handle it."

He gave her another one of those long, thoughtful looks he'd been tossing her way over the past twenty-four hours, as if he were assessing her. She had a feeling his initial impression of her had changed quite a bit since he dragged her out of that parking lot into the woods, with good reason. The woman he knew was Susannah Marsh, a sophisticated, polished professional.

But the woman standing here in jeans and sneakers was all Susan McKenzie, except for the brunette dye job. She wore no makeup, her gray eyes were back to their normal color, and she even carried herself differently, her shoulders squared to challenge an unforgiving world.

She was her grandmother's granddaughter, after all.

"Okay," Hunter said finally with a brief nod. "I'll get the pack."

"I'll see what we can take with us from the pantry."

As she started to pass him, he reached out and touched her hand. A brief flick of his fingers against hers, but it was enough to send tremors darting down her spine. She looked up, not feeling nearly as fierce as she had just a moment earlier, and the heat that poured into her belly at the look in his eyes only made her feel weak-kneed and vulnerable.

"I know you don't trust me," he said quietly. "I know you have no reason to. But I take protecting you very seriously. I don't want you to be afraid of me."

"I'm not." She forced her chin up, even though she was feeling anything but strong.

"Good." His fingers brushed hers one more time, the lightest of caresses, and fell away.

Somehow, she managed to make it to the kitchen without her wobbly knees buckling under her.

Chapter Ten

About four months earlier, shortly after Alexander Quinn had approached him at Smoky Joe's Saloon in Bitterwood, Hunter had decided to see what the CEO of The Gates was really all about. So he'd followed the man one afternoon on a winding ride up Lamentation Rise, a foothill just outside the Great Smoky Mountain National Park. On a clear day, he suspected, a person could probably see most of Ridge County spread out like a postcard, but the day he'd followed Quinn had been rainy and cool for early June. The peak had seemed to be buried in the clouds, the sprawling cabin near the summit a misty apparition in the afternoon gloom.

All this time, Hunter had believed that Quinn hadn't spotted his tail job. He should have known better.

"Meet me at my cabin on Lamentation Rise," Quinn had said tersely into the phone after warning Hunter about the two men heading for his front door. "I know you know where that is."

"How much farther?" Trudging beside Hunter, Susannah sounded weary. She looked weary as well, her brow furrowed and dark circles starting to bruise the skin beneath her winter-gray eyes. They'd been hiking for almost two hours now, rabbiting around in circles for the first mile up to be sure to avoid any searchers out in the woods. Quinn's cabin was far enough up the mountain that it wasn't likely the searchers would get anywhere near it.

But they had to get there without being spotted first.

"Almost there," he told her, hoping he was telling the truth. Quinn had given him quick GPS coordinates before hanging up, but a lot had been going on. He wasn't sure he'd remembered them exactly, and it wouldn't take much to go completely off track.

If he could just find the narrow road he'd traveled up the mountain to reach Quinn's cabin—

"Is that a road?" Susannah asked.

He followed her gaze and saw the dusty gray of a gravel track barely visible through the trees ahead.

"It is," he answered, relief fluttering in his gut. Reaching for her hand and giving it a tug, he set out for the road, giving her little choice but to follow.

The day was clear, the cabin visible almost as soon as they reached the rocky road up the rise. Next to Hunter, Susannah sucked in a quick breath, and he turned to find her grimacing.

The gravel, he realized, watching her take a couple of limping steps forward. The rocky surface must be hell on her injured feet, especially after so much nonstop hiking.

He shrugged his pack from his back and swung it from the crook of one elbow. "Okay. Hop on." He held his free hand out to her.

She looked at him as if he'd lost his mind. "You've got to be kidding."

"You enjoy pain?"

"*Enjoy* might be a strong word. I can endure it, though."

"You don't have to. Come on. Piggyback time."

She stared at him a moment, her lips pressed into a thin line of annoyance. But he could see the idea of getting off her sore feet appealed to her as well.

"Oh, what the hell." She grabbed his shoulders and jumped onto his back, wrapping her legs around his waist. "Mush!"

Grinning, he hooked his arm around her legs to steady her and carried her forward. The extra weight of the woman and her pack made the last few yards to the cabin downright grueling, but he made it there without any embarrassing stumbles and deposited her on the first step of the cabin's wooden porch.

Before he had a chance to catch his breath, the front door of the cabin opened and Alexander Quinn stepped out onto the porch, greeting them with a silent nod.

Susannah's surprised gaze flicked toward Hunter. "What's going on?"

"Susannah, this is Alexander Quinn. Quinn, this is Susannah Marsh."

Quinn's eyes narrowed slightly at the introduction, but he managed a hint of a smile as he reached out his hand. "Ms. Marsh."

Hunter watched as the princess reappeared, her neck extending regally and her movement graceful as she took Quinn's hand and shook it firmly. "Mr. Quinn."

Quinn's lips quirked at the corners but the smile faded as quickly as it had come. He released Susannah's hand and looked at Hunter. "Any trouble getting here?"

"We had to do some evasive maneuvers on the way up, but no trouble."

Quinn took the pack from Hunter's arm and motioned for Susannah to give him her backpack as well. "Hungry?"

Susannah's eyes lit up before she could school her features to a neutral mask.

"Food would be great," Hunter answered for her, following her and Quinn into the cabin.

While the large cabin was rustic-looking on the outside, inside Quinn had made the most of the space to showcase an exotic display of furniture, fabrics and knickknacks he'd apparently collected during decades of Foreign Service. Hunter supposed the princess, who was looking around the place with great interest, could probably tell him just what it was he was looking at as he scanned the room and drank in the riot of color and textures, but all he could think about was finding the nearest tub and taking a long, hot soak.

His bum leg felt as if it were about to fall right off his body.

"I have to be back at the office in an hour, so we don't have long," Quinn warned as he deposited the backpacks near the large brown leather sofa that took up most of the middle of the large front room. "The fridge is full, so as soon as we have a quick word about tomorrow, you can dig in and see what you like."

"Tomorrow?" Susannah and Hunter asked in unison.

Quinn looked up at them both. "Tomorrow is the start of the conference. And we're going to have to figure out a way to get the two of you back in that hotel."

Hunter was used to his boss's bluntness by now, but he'd have expected Susannah to bristle. Instead, she gave a short nod and said, "I've had a thought about that."

Even more interesting was Quinn's lack of reaction to Susannah's response, as if she'd behaved exactly as he expected. And there'd been that considering look earlier when Hunter had introduced him.

Just what did Quinn know about Susannah that Hunter didn't?

"THERE'S A SKELETON crew after midnight, so if we're going to get into the hotel before the conference starts, tonight's our best bet." Susannah peered at the hotel floor plans that Quinn had produced when they gathered around the small round table in the kitchen. The cabin was deliciously warm—central heating rather than wall units—and on her way from the front room to the kitchen, she'd glimpsed a large bathroom she couldn't wait to try out.

But first things first.

"The entrance from the executive parking garage leads into the basement level, which is maintenance and storage." She pointed to the floor plans. "There's an elevator here, but it's noisy when it reaches a floor and opens, so we'd lose any advantage of stealth. Plus, it's like being stuck in a cage—if there's someone waiting at the floor we exit, we're busted. I think our best bet is to bypass the elevators and take the stairs."

Across the table from her, Hunter grimaced. He'd been favoring his left leg since they'd arrived at Quinn's cabin, the limp more noticeable. She felt a twinge of guilt about letting him carry her on his back. All she had were some scrapes and bruises on her feet. He probably had bullet shrapnel and God only knew how much surgical hardware in that bad leg of his.

They were going to be quite the cat-burgling pair tonight.

"What's the plan when we get upstairs?" Hunter asked in a lazy drawl that belied the sharpness of his gaze.

"First, I'd like to take a look inside Marcus Lemonde's desk," Susannah replied.

"You think he'd keep something incriminating there?" Quinn asked.

She slanted a look his way. "I don't know. I'll tell you more once I've searched it."

"How're you going to get into the office?" Quinn asked. "Isn't it locked at night?"

And her keys were somewhere with her purse, wherever she'd dropped it during the ambush. "I didn't think of that."

"I did," Hunter said with a grin. "I made a copy

of your office key from the master set at the hotel once I realized you were the BRI's target."

"So that's how you got my clothing and shoe sizes." She wasn't sure whether she was impressed by his resourcefulness or a bit creeped out by the fact that he'd gone through her things thoroughly enough to find the change of clothes she kept in the bathroom closet in her office.

"Do you know anything about handling firearms?" Quinn asked Susannah.

"I do," she answered. "I'm best with a Remington 700."

"A bit big for our purposes," Hunter murmured, giving her an odd look.

What's the matter, big guy? You think a girl can't handle a big gun? She shot him a hard look. "I've handled pistols, too. My personal weapon is a Ruger SR40."

Hunter's green eyes glinted amusement. "The princess has teeth."

Princess?

"I have a Glock 27 I think you can use with no problems." Quinn crossed to a large armoire near the fireplace and unlocked it to reveal a gun cabinet. There were rifles, pistols, shotguns, even a couple of high-tech hunting crossbows. From the drawers in the middle of the armoire, he pulled a box of .40-caliber ammunition. "This should do you for tonight." He handed over the pistol and the ammo.

"I've got my Glock," Hunter said, "and some rounds in the backpack, but if I need more, you have any 9 mm rounds?" The look Quinn gave him made Hunter laugh. "Right. Who do I think I'm talking to?"

"I have to go. Can't be late for this meeting." Quinn was already on his way toward the door. He stopped at the entrance and turned to look at them. "Consider this your place for now. I'll be staying in town. There's a Ford Explorer in the garage out back. I left the keys for you on the dresser in the master bedroom, along with a new burner phone. Call if you need me—my secure number is already listed on the speed dial." His gaze wandered from Hunter to Susannah. "I'll let you two work out the sleeping arrangements."

Then he was gone, the door closing firmly behind him.

"He has a lot of faith in you," Susannah remarked.

"Looks like he has some faith in you as well." Hunter turned to look at her, his eyes narrowed with suspicion. "Do you know each other?"

She shook her head. "Never met him before."

"He seems to know a lot more about you than I do."

Hunter's words set off a flutter of alarm in her

belly. She tried to quell it, taking care that her expression showed none of her sudden apprehension. "There's not a lot to know."

"Somehow I doubt that," he murmured.

"Do you mind if I take the bathroom first?" She started moving toward the hall without waiting for him to answer.

Before they'd settled down with the hotel floor plans, Quinn had told her he'd put some clothes for them both in the closet of the master bedroom and had pointed out the door on their way to the kitchen. She detoured to the master bedroom to pick out a change of clothes and stopped short in the doorway.

The room was larger than she'd expected, big enough to accommodate a huge king-size bed, a dresser and chest of drawers, and a sitting area near an enormous wall of windows that overlooked miles of cloud-capped mountains to the east. It was the view that caught her breath, and she made her way to the large-paned windows, wondering just how much Alexander Quinn had paid for a view this amazing.

"I thought you were headed to the bathroom." Hunter's low voice was so close she jumped. He put his hands on her shoulders to steady her, smiling a little as she turned to face him. "Sorry. Didn't mean to startle you."

"This place must have cost a fortune," she said,

nodding toward the window. "You don't get a view like that for cheap."

His hands still warm on her shoulders, he followed her gaze. "I guess so. I don't think Quinn's hurting for money."

She wasn't inclined to remind him he was still touching her, since she was in no hurry for him to stop. "I guess The Gates is pretty successful, then?"

He shrugged. "I haven't been working there long. I don't think it's even been in business that long, come to think of it. Maybe it's family money."

"Or whatever alphabet-soup job he had before opening his agency paid better than we thought."

He looked at her then. "Alphabet-soup job?"

"You know, FBI, NSA, CIA, something like that. He has covert operative written all over him, don't you think?" Which might explain why he seemed to know more about her than she liked.

What if he knew exactly who she was? It was possible, she supposed; the situation that had sent her running to her aunt's home in Raleigh had made the papers as far away as Nashville and Chattanooga, she knew. And Alexander Quinn came across as a man who made a point of knowing everything there was to know about anyone who crossed his professional path. Once he knew she was a target, he'd have looked into her past.

How far back had he been able to go?

She'd changed her look in the twelve years since she'd left Boneyard Ridge. Different eye color—at least, until she'd lost the contacts. She had a different hair color and hairstyle. Gone were the faded, sometimes ratty jeans and tees she'd worn most days, now replaced by stylish tailored suits and stratospheric heels. Makeup and polished manners helped her look like a completely different creature, but at her core, she was still Susan McKenzie, a little redneck girl from the hillbilly haven of Boneyard Ridge.

She supposed someone like Alexander Quinn, who'd clearly spent a little time dealing with people who lied for a living, could see through her facade easily enough to know she wasn't who she appeared to be.

But what other secrets had he learned?

Hunter dropped his hands from her shoulders, and she bit back a sigh of disappointment. It wasn't a good idea to get used to having him around. Not good to start thinking about other places he could touch her, either. They would get through this mess tonight, and then she'd have to get serious about coming up with a different name, a different look and a different place to hide.

She'd taken a lot of risks coming here to Barrowville, so close to her hometown just across the county line.

She should have known better.

But she'd missed the mountains, living in the city. In the flatlands, as she and other hill folks called it. She hadn't been meant to live in the flatlands, especially not in a sprawling, noisy capital city like Raleigh, North Carolina. The job offer at the Highland Hotel and Resort had seemed like a kiss from God himself.

But everything had changed now. Once she was done here, it would be time to move on again.

Hunter wandered over to the closet. "Want to take bets on whether he got our sizes right?" he drawled.

"I'd bet on Quinn." She turned to watch as he pulled out a couple of large suitcases and hauled them up onto the bed.

The CEO of The Gates had done more than select the right sizes. He'd also chosen exactly the clothing she'd have opted for herself in the same situation—sturdy jeans, shirts and sweaters that would easily layer, and a weather-resistant coat that would keep her both warm and dry if she and Hunter were forced to brave the elements again after their hotel caper. Nothing stylish or decorative in the lot. Certainly nothing Susannah Marsh would have chosen for herself.

But Susan McKenzie, on the other hand—

"How'd he do?" Hunter asked, pulling out a pair of boxers, a long-sleeved tee and a pair of jeans from his own clothing stash.

"Not bad," she answered. "How about you?"

"Everything looks like it'll fit." He nodded toward a door next to the closet. "I think that's probably a bathroom, if you'd like a little more privacy. I can take the other bathroom."

She opened the door and found a roomy if utilitarian bathroom behind it, complete with a large tub and a separate shower. "Okay, thanks." She turned to smile at him, but he was already halfway out the door.

Tamping down a sigh, she dug out a fresh change of clothes and headed for the shower.

THE WATER JETS in the whirlpool bath shot warm bursts of water against his aching leg, easing the tension in his muscles and sending little shivers of relief jolting through him. Leaning back against the foot of the tub, Hunter closed his eyes and tried to clear his mind of his escalating list of troubles and concerns. The key to a successful mission, he knew, was laser focus on the ultimate goal.

Tonight's goal wasn't to get in and out of the Highland Hotel and Resort undetected. That was just the means to the end. Nor was the goal to discover exactly what Billy Dawson and his crew

were planning for the law-enforcement conference that started the next day, although that was
also on their agenda.

No, the goal was to stop the BRI's plan before
it ever started. And that meant they were going
to have to think like terrorists.

Hunter had some experience with getting
into the heads of people who thought nothing of
blowing up hundreds or thousands of civilians to
achieve their goals. The mind of a terrorist was a
bleak, soulless place. He didn't imagine it made
much difference what the terrorist's goal might
be—anyone who gave no thought to differentiat-
ing between innocent civilians and armed troops
was a monster. Any deviation was a matter of
degree, not intent.

The BRI had already proved their depravity by
going after Susannah Marsh. The woman meant
nothing to them, other than the impediment she
posed to their plans for the conference. She was
nothing more than a lock to be broken, moved
aside and discarded.

Don't think about her. She's a distraction.

But he could hardly shut her from his mind,
could he? She wasn't merely a target to be protected. She was going to be his partner in this
break-in, and if he didn't take hold of his libido
when she was around, this mission would go
straight to hell.

When the hot water and whirlpool motion finally unknotted his muscles enough to erase the worst of the pain and fatigue in his bum leg, he drained the tub, toweled himself dry and went to look for Susannah.

He found her in the front room, hunched on the sofa in front of the television that hung over the fireplace. She'd dressed in jeans and a dark blue sweater that hugged her lithe body like a lover. But what he saw on her face as she watched the screen quelled any prurient urges he might have indulged.

She looked terrified.

He followed her gaze to the television screen and saw that she was watching a midday news program out of Knoxville. As an attractive blond news anchor spoke, the image on the screen changed to a slightly grainy photo of Susannah. She looked pretty and composed in what must have been her official publicity headshot, a Mona Lisa smile barely hinting at the depths of the woman beneath the placid exterior.

"As authorities widen their search for the missing Barrowville woman, the mystery surrounding her deepens. Who is Susannah Marsh? Authorities aren't willing to discuss anything about her background on the record, but sources close to the investigation admit they're stymied in their attempts to learn more about the missing woman's murky past."

Hunter turned his gaze back to Susannah's stricken face. Her eyes were closed, her lips trembling.

"Who is Susannah Marsh?" he asked softly, crossing to sit on the sturdy coffee table in front of the sofa.

She opened her eyes slowly, her eyes dark with fear.

"A lie," she said.

Chapter Eleven

"I was sixteen." The words seemed to squeeze their way from her tight throat, past her reluctant tongue and lips, to spill into the taut silence of Alexander Quinn's cabin. She opened her eyes to find Hunter's green-eyed gaze fixed on her face, serious but somehow comforting, as if he wanted only to understand her.

She wanted to believe there was someone she could trust with the real truth about who she was, because it had been a long, long time since she'd revealed anything true about herself to anyone.

"You were sixteen," he prodded gently when her nerves failed her.

She reached across the space between them, squeezing his hand. "You have to promise me you'll never tell another soul what I'm about to say. Promise me."

His brow furrowed. "Did you kill someone?"

Her whole body went numb, and she jerked her hand away.

He caught her arms in his big, strong hands as she started to rise. "Tell me, Susannah. Tell me what has you so damn scared."

"I can't."

"I won't tell another soul what you tell me. I don't care what it is. I swear it." His fingers cupped her chin, forced her to look at him. His green eyes were solemn. "I won't tell anyone."

"If you do, you might as well put a gun to my head and pull the trigger." She hated how melodramatic those words sounded, how overwrought. But the truth was the truth.

"I told you. Not a word." He dropped his hand away from her face, let go of her arm and sat back, giving her space, as if he understood just how vulnerable she felt at the moment.

She swallowed with difficulty and began again. "My whole life, until I was sixteen, I lived in a place called Boneyard Ridge, just across the county line from here. It's a little nothing of a place, not much more than a road curving over a mountain, a few homes dotting the ridge. Most everybody who had a lick of sense or two pennies to rub together got out as soon as they could, but my grandmother had no intention of going anywhere. 'I was born here, and here I'll meet my Maker,' she always said. I used to think she was crazy. Until I had to leave the place myself."

"Had to leave."

She looked up at him, trying to read his thoughts behind his placid green eyes. "When I was sixteen, a man named Clinton Bradbury decided I was going to be his, and I'd have no say about it. I never gave him any encouragement, no matter what the Bradburys told folks. But he wanted what he wanted, and I don't know why, but he wanted me. I told him no a dozen times, but he thought I could be broken. He threatened my grandmother, which he should've known better than to do."

"What did she do?"

"Ran him off our property with a shotgun and told him never to come back."

"But he did?"

She nodded, unable to meet his gaze. "My grandmother had fallen down the stairs at the church that morning and they wanted to keep her at the hospital over in Maryville overnight for observation. She didn't want me to stay at the cabin by myself, but I told her I could take care of myself. I was nearly grown up, you know? And Clinton hadn't come around again since the shotgun incident."

"But he came that night."

"He'd been waitin' for the chance." She heard the way her accent broadened and hardened into the mountain cadence she'd spent years trying to erase. She sighed. "He just didn't know I had a shotgun of my own."

Silence fell between them for a long, thick moment before she could find her voice again. "I shot him just the once, but it was close range and true. I guess I hit an artery, 'cause before I knew it, there was an ocean of blood on my bedroom floor."

Hunter reached across the space between them and closed his hand over her arm. Her skin rippled beneath his touch, but she didn't let herself pull away. "I'm sorry," he murmured. "That must have been awful for you."

"I didn't want him dead. I just wanted him to stop. I tried to talk him out of there, but he wouldn't listen. He kept grabbing me. He tore my pajama pants—" She shuddered at the memory, at the rage and sense of violation that haunted her to this day. "I couldn't let him rape me. I just couldn't. I didn't have a lot in the world, but my body was my own and I hadn't agreed to give it to him."

"The police didn't believe you?"

She looked up quickly. "We'd already talked to the sheriff about the way Clinton had been harassing us. We'd made reports, played it by the book. Let's just say, they weren't surprised."

"Then why did you have to run?"

"The sheriff isn't the real power in Boneyard

Ridge." Her voice lowered with anger. "That would be the Bradburys. And they didn't care what Clinton had done to earn that load of buckshot. They just knew one of their kinfolk was dead, and I'd done it." She could still hear old Abel Bradbury's rough-edged voice. "You don't kill a Bradbury in Boneyard Ridge and get away with it."

"So you had to hide from them."

"If I wanted to live. They damn near killed me once already." She pulled aside the neckline of her sweater and showed him a bullet scar that marred her skin just above her left collarbone.

Hunter muttered a profanity.

"The cops couldn't find the person who took a potshot at me right outside my own door. If my grandmother hadn't been there, if she hadn't dragged me inside before they could get off another shot—" She wrapped her arms around herself, even though she no longer felt cold. "The cops never found the rifle that shot me, so they couldn't tie the shooting to the Bradburys."

"A lot of places in the hills to hide your sins."

She nodded. "But I knew who shot me. Besides my grandmother, nobody else in Boneyard Ridge gave a damn about me one way or another. Nobody but the Bradburys, and they just wanted me dead."

Hunter touched her cheek. She tried not to

flinch, but it was too soon, her emotions too raw, to handle the feel of his fingers on her flesh. He dropped his hand away. "I'm sorry."

She shook her head. "It's not you. I promise, it's nothing to do with you. It's just—" She stopped short, her gaze sliding toward the now muted television, where the news had ended and a judge show had begun. She reached for the remote on the table beside Hunter and turned off the television. "I look different now. I do. I dyed my hair brown and started wearing it long, and I wore those brown contacts. I changed the way I talk, the way I walk, the way I hold my head, the way I think. I changed my name, legally. I've kept to myself, made no close friendships, never let myself get involved with a man who might want to know more about my past. And for twelve years now, I've managed to avoid detection by the Bradburys."

"But hiding in a crowd is one thing. Hiding when your face has been splashed on the news—"

"I look different," she repeated. "Just not different enough."

"You're going to have to run again."

She nodded. "They'll know the name I'm going by now. They can find out where I was living. I can't go back there now, can't get any of my things. I have to leave everything behind. My savings, what few keepsakes I've allowed myself." She bit her lower lip until it hurt, but she managed to keep the tears at bay. "Good thing I never got that cat I've been wanting, huh?"

He reached toward her again, his hand stilling midair before dropping back to his lap. "Maybe you don't have to keep running."

She stared at him. "Didn't you hear anything I just said?"

"You're alone. So you run."

"Yes."

"What if you weren't alone?"

"But I *am* alone. I have to be alone."

This time, he did touch her, his big, rough hand closing over hers. "No. You don't."

The conviction in his voice sliced into her heart like a razor. "Hunter, no. There's nothing you or anyone else can do."

"I was a soldier, remember? Protecting people is what I did. It's still what I do. It's what I'm doing right now."

"You can't protect me 24/7. You have a life. A job."

"So I make you my job."

"That sounds terrible."

One corner of his lip quirked. "For you or for me?"

She turned her hand over, pressing her palm to his. "For you. And for me. I can't live my life in a cage or wrapped up in cotton batting like a piece of china stored in a drawer. And I could never ask you to make my safety your priority."

"You didn't ask. I offered."

"Because you're a soldier with nobody to protect." She felt a surge of emotion at the thought, equal parts admiration and pity. "You don't know how to be anything else, do you?"

His green eyes darkened, and he looked away. "You don't know me."

"I don't. And I don't reckon you know me, either. And that's why I could never ask you to put your life on hold to protect mine."

He slid his hand from her grasp. "It's not right that you have to run. You did nothing to deserve it."

"I killed a man."

"Who was trying to rape you."

"Be that as it may, I killed him. It's on my soul, whether he deserved it or not." She tried to push aside the memory of Clinton Bradbury's body bleeding out on her bedroom floor. "I'm not willing to give my life as penance, no. But I'm sure as hell not willing to give anyone else's life, either."

"Well," he said, lifting his gaze to meet hers, "what happened to you years ago changes nothing about tonight, does it? We still have a job to do, and if we get caught by the wrong people while we're doing it, what the Bradburys want to do to you may not matter, anyway."

He was right about that much. The Bradburys, while a threat hanging over her head for over a decade, weren't her most pressing concern.

The Blue Ridge Infantry and their plans for the conference tomorrow were. And instead of sitting here feeling sorry for herself, she should be focusing her attention on how they were going to get inside the hotel without being caught— and what they were going to do once they were inside.

She and Hunter rose at the same time, their bodies gliding into each other and tangling for a long, breathless moment. She reached out to steady herself, her palm flattening against the solid, hot wall of his chest. Beneath her fingers, his heartbeat stuttered and began to gallop, as if racing to catch up with the sudden acceleration of her own pulse. His arm roped around her waist, tugging her closer, and in the glimmer of his green eyes she saw fierce, feral intent that should have frightened her. But it didn't.

It thrilled her.

His thighs pressed against hers, driving her back toward the sofa. She wrapped one arm around his shoulders to keep from falling, drawing him even closer. His breath heated her cheeks, his grip tightening as he held her in place.

She should pull away from him. Put distance

between them, between what he was offering and what she could afford to have.

But as his gaze dipped to her lips, and he tugged her body flat against his, she couldn't move. Couldn't think about anything at all but how strongly, how desperately she needed to know what it was like to kiss him.

She imagined his kiss would be fierce and demanding, as strong and relentless as she knew from experience he could be. But what she hadn't reckoned on, what shocked her lips apart and sent her heart rate hurtling toward oblivion as his lips claimed hers, was the tenderness that trembled beneath all that tightly leashed passion.

He might not know her, but he knew exactly what she needed, as if he'd looked deep down in her well-buried heart and saw all the secret longings that writhed there, desperate for discovery.

His fingers threaded through her hair, holding her still as he slanted his head to deepen the kiss. His tongue swept over hers, setting off fireworks behind her closed eyelids, and she dug her fingers into the stone-hard muscles of his chest just to keep from tumbling off balance. When he dragged his lips from hers, she couldn't seem to breathe for a long, shivering moment.

"We have to focus." His voice came out in a raspy growl as he edged clear of her, retreating to a spot near the windows.

She groped for the arm of the sofa and perched there before her trembling knees gave out from under her. "Right."

He was breathing hard, as if they'd just hiked up Lamentation Rise again. As if he'd carried her on his back the whole way. But after a few seconds, the harsh sounds subsided, and as she watched, he visibly composed himself, a soldier packing his kit until it was pin-neat.

"I've got something I need to do," he told her. "Can you start packing our rucksacks? We need food for three days, in case we have to run for it and can't get back here. Lightweight as you can make it."

She nodded. "What's the one more thing you have to do?"

He flashed her a brief, mysterious smile. "You'll see soon enough." He headed down the hall and disappeared into the bathroom.

"IT'S HER, ISN'T IT?"

Asa Bradbury turned his attention from the television screen hanging over the bar and looked at his cousin Ricky. He should be feeling triumph, he supposed, at having found her after more than a decade of searching, but there wasn't really much pleasure in finally tracking down the girl. None of it would bring Clinton back. And, if Asa was honest with himself, he hadn't missed the trouble that seemed to follow Clinton around like a viperous pet, leaving nothing but havoc in his wake.

But family honor was family honor, and the girl had killed one of his kinsmen. Letting her go unpunished was neither wise nor proper, not if he wanted the Bradbury name to mean anything in these hills.

"What are we going to do about it?" Ricky asked.

Asa slanted a gaze at the younger man, disappointed that he'd even felt the need to ask the question. "We're going to find her, of course."

There was no other option.

IT HAD BEEN a year and three months since he'd worn his hair high and tight. Since he'd been completely clean-shaven and spit-polished. His so-called comrades in the Blue Ridge Infantry had never seen him looking like anything more than the down-on-his-luck, chip-on-his-shoulder Army washout he'd presented to them.

The man in the mirror was achingly familiar, a face he'd seen thousands of times in the past twelve years. A man of honor and purpose.

But somehow, the face staring back at him remained a stranger, far removed from who he'd become since his world blew up around him in a valley in Afghanistan.

Fraud, he thought, staring back at the familiar stranger. *Poser.*

He looked away, squaring his shoulders and lifting his smooth-shaven chin toward the bathroom door. He could afford to be neither, not when there was a woman out there with the soul of a warrior who needed him to watch her back. He had to figure out how to be a soldier again, at least for a few more days.

He could do that, couldn't he?

He found Susannah in the kitchen, packing what looked like protein bars, small tins of meat and bottles of water into the backpacks. She glanced up as he entered, did a double take that made him smile, then turned fully toward him, her head cocked and her lips quirked in a bemused half smile.

"Well, hello, soldier," she murmured.

"That's Army First Sergeant Bragg to you, ma'am," he shot back with a grin he almost felt.

Leaving the rucksacks on the table, she made a slow circle around him, observing his new look from all angles. "I think I approve."

"I was holding my breath."

The grin she flashed his way felt like a shot of adrenaline blazing straight to his gut. He felt his spine straighten to attention, along with a quickening somewhere south of his backbone.

Bringing himself back under control with the

speed of the well-trained warrior he used to be, he nodded at the packs. "Anything else we need?"

She showed him what she'd included—food, lightweight tools, more first-aid supplies, even a folded map of Tennessee. "In case we need to make a run for it, at least we'll have some idea where we are when we get there."

"Good thinking." He zipped up one of the sacks and slung it over one shoulder. "How are your feet?"

She looked down at the tennis shoes she wore. "They hurt. But I'll deal. How's your leg?"

"Still held together with nuts and bolts. I'll deal, too."

Cocking her head, she let her gaze fall to his left leg, her scrutiny intense and disconcerting. "What's under there, exactly?"

He considered and rejected a salacious retort, knowing that such an obvious attempt at distraction would only make her more curious. "Some missing muscle tissue. A lot of scarring."

"Can I see it?" Almost as soon as the words slipped from her mouth, her gaze snapped up to meet his, a flush of pink color darkening her face. "I'm sorry. I did not just ask you that."

"I think you did," he answered, stunned by the fact that he was actually standing here in the middle of Alexander Quinn's kitchen, seriously considering dropping trou so she could see his bum leg.

All because she'd asked him to do it.

"I just—" She pressed her lips to a thin line, her brow furrowing. "I don't know why, but I want to know—"

"What it looks like?"

She shook her head, still frowning. "It's not curiosity. It's—" She blew out a long breath. "Never mind. Forget I said anything."

Perversely, her change of heart only made him want to show her what his jeans were hiding. It wasn't pretty. It might even be shocking—there were still days, even now, when he looked at his scarred leg and cringed at the sight.

But it would be honest. As honest as the moment when she'd looked up at him with those big gray eyes and confessed she'd killed a man with a shotgun.

Before he lost his nerve, he unzipped his jeans and pulled them down, baring his bad leg to her searching eyes.

Chapter Twelve

Susannah's gaze flicked down toward the road map of scars that circled his leg from thigh to ankle. Her mouth dropped open and she released a shaky gasp.

Hunter followed her gaze, trying to remember what it had been like to get that first look at his injury. It had been so much worse then, of course, the edges of torn skin raw and discolored and barely held together with hundreds of sutures.

Even now, with the wounds long healed, the contours of the leg were misshapen in places where the blast had destroyed muscle tissue. There was one particularly large patch of skin on his calf where doctors had used skin grafts to repair the damage from a large piece of flaming debris. And the scars were still purple and angry-looking, potent reminders of the horrors of that day in the Helmand Province.

"Oh," she said. The word came out long and slow, like a lament.

He reached for his jeans and started to pull them back up, but in the span of a heartbeat, she was at his side, her fingers brushing over the long scar on his thigh with exquisite delicacy.

"Does it hurt?" she asked softly, her gaze lingering on the scar.

"No," he lied. It hurt, horribly, but not the way she meant.

And even worse, her fingers on his flesh felt as good as anything he'd experienced in a long, long time. So good that every inch of his skin, even the broken patches that were still partly numb, seemed to burst into flames at her touch.

"I can't believe I let you haul me around on your back."

He pulled away from her pity, dragging his jeans back into place and zipping the fly with trembling fingers.

"I didn't mean—" She broke off midsentence, frustration evident in her pale eyes. "I'm sorry. I shouldn't have—"

"No. I shouldn't have." He scraped his hand through his hair, shocked by how effortlessly it ran across the short spikes of his newly shaved cut.

"You don't think it makes you less—" Once again, she stopped short.

He made himself look at her and saw her gazing back at him with a look so full of misery that he felt like a heel.

"Less what? Less virile? Less of a man?"

"Do you?"

He didn't know how to answer that question. The injury certainly hadn't done a damn thing to quell his sex drive, if his current state of arousal was any indication.

But he hadn't had sex since the injury. Never even really considered it seriously, not to this day.

And he was pretty sure the mangled condition of his leg figured into that equation somewhere.

"I know guys aren't as sensitive as women about their looks," she said quietly. She still stood close to him, close enough to touch. Close enough to catch fire if the flames surging inside him broke loose of his faltering control.

"Probably not," he admitted. "I'm not ashamed of my scars."

He was ashamed of what had led to them, however. If he was being perfectly honest with himself, a circumstance he mostly avoided these days. Honesty was painful, and he was tired of hurting.

"You shouldn't be."

He wanted to argue with her, the urge to spill the whole ugly tale so powerful it felt like poison in his gut. His leg was bad. It couldn't do the same things he'd once asked of it. But he was stronger now than he had been in the middle of that burning hell.

He'd never known that level of utter helplessness before in his life. He prayed to God he'd never know it again.

He willed Susannah to step back from him, to take away her soft warmth, her sweet scent, her gentle, disarming gaze.

Of course, being Susannah, she stepped closer, her hands lifting to his cheeks, ensnaring him. "I have no idea what to say to you," she said, her voice a whisper. "I don't know what you need."

You, he thought with growing dismay. *I just need you.*

When she leaned in, he thought she was going to kiss him. But then her face turned, her cheek glided like silk against his, and she pulled him into an embrace that threatened to deconstruct him completely.

He tried not to return the embrace, tried not to let his arms wrap around her slim waist and tug her closer, tried not to bury his face in the curve of her neck. Tried not to need her so desperately.

He did not succeed.

Time seemed to slow to nothing, and still she didn't move away from him. They settled there, his hips pressed back into the kitchen counter, her legs tangled with his as she settled her body against his. Despite his arousal, he felt no burning need to change anything, no desire to break away from her grasp nor to take control and push the closeness between them to a different place.

Slowly, the tension in his body eased, and even desire ebbed to a slow, sweet burn low in his belly. He felt her fingers brush through the crisp stubble of his buzz cut, exploring lightly, like a curious child.

A bubble of humor rose unexpectedly in his chest. "The ladies always love the buzz cut," he murmured against her throat.

She laughed in his ear, but he felt it rumble through him everywhere their bodies touched. "It's hypnotic."

He eased her away from him, but not too far, still holding on to her waist to keep her close. "In case you're wondering, my virility is just fine."

She flashed him a sly grin. "Yeah, I can tell."

She crossed back to the table, picked up her own pack and slipped her arms through the straps, adjusting them until they fit. By the time she put the backpack down and turned to face him again, she'd donned a mask of cool professionalism, as if the warm, sweet woman who'd just hugged him out of his bad mood had disappeared.

He felt the loss more keenly than he'd expected.

"I think we're going to have to risk leaving the packs somewhere off the hotel property," she said. "If we take them with us, we'll stick out like sore thumbs, and I don't like the idea of leaving them in the SUV, in case we can't get back to the parking garage."

"Good thinking." He flashed her a grin. "Sure you didn't spend some time in the Army?"

She smiled, but there was careful distance in her expression. "I'm sure. But I think my grandmother may have spent some time as a boot-camp drill sergeant."

There was a thread of sadness in her voice, underlying the composure. It had sharp edges, pricking his conscience. He'd spent so much of the last few months with his head stuck in the middle of his own problems, it hadn't even occurred to him that she had spent over a decade isolated from everyone she'd loved. "Do you ever get to see your grandmother?"

She looked away, her profile sharp with regret. "She died two years ago." She turned her winter-bleak eyes to meet his gaze. "We made a deal before I left, you see. That she would take out a classified ad in the online Knoxville newspaper once a week, just to let me know everything was okay. Then, one month, it wasn't there. And I knew. I checked the obituaries for the month and there it was. She died peacefully in her sleep at the age of eighty-nine."

Despite the distance she'd deliberately put between them, he couldn't have stopped himself from touching her again if he'd tried. Cradling her face between his hands, he bent and kissed her forehead. "I'm sorry. I would hate to find out about my sister's death that way."

She covered his hands with hers, gently easing them away from her face and stepping back. But she kept her fingers entwined with his. "Does your sister know? What you're doing? Where you are?"

Her question was as good as a bucket of ice water in the face. Janet knew he'd joined the BRI. But she didn't know he was working undercover. Quinn had convinced him he couldn't let her know the truth.

Now he wished he'd listened to his own instincts. But he couldn't dwell on what he couldn't change.

Avoiding the question, he let go of her fingers and nodded toward the back door. The garage that held their transportation was through that door. "Let's get everything packed in the SUV for tonight. Then we should probably try to get some sleep. It's going to be a long night."

Without waiting for her, he headed out the cabin's back door.

SHE SHOULD BE feeling anxious, Susannah thought. Jittery. But somehow the mere act of doing something besides running and hiding had a calming effect on her nerves, so that by the time they pulled up to the ticket gate of the executive parking garage, she rattled off the employee access code without even having to think about it, though it had been months since she'd parked there.

"Will hotel security be able to identify you by the code?" Hunter asked a moment later as the metal gate rose and they drove into the belly of the concrete garage.

"No. It's a universal code. They do change it whenever an executive leaves or is fired, but there's not a lot of turnover here. The company treats executives well, and it's hard to beat the view from our offices."

"I didn't spot a camera, but I assume there is one?"

"I honestly don't know. Like I said, security expenditures tend to lean heavily on the guest-protection side of the equation. If there is a camera, it's probably not great quality." She glanced at him, taking in his pin-neat appearance. "And trust me when I say, even up close, you look nothing like the maintenance man I ran into in the elevator the other day."

The corner of his lip crooked. "Should I say thanks?"

She grinned back at him. "Entirely up to you."

He picked out a parking spot halfway between the exit and the basement entrance, close enough that they had a chance of winning a footrace to the SUV but not so close that they'd have to drive the whole curving length of the garage to reach freedom.

They'd stashed their rucksacks behind a fallen tree about a quarter mile up the winding two-lane road that led to the Highland Hotel and Resort. If they managed to ditch pursuers by the time they reached that spot in the road, they could pull off down a dirt road about two hundred yards past the hiding place, hide the SUV in the trees and circle back to get their supplies.

For the hotel invasion, they'd agreed to take a minimum of tools. Their weapons, of course— Hunter's Glock still safely hidden in his ankle holster, hers tucked into a pancake holster at the small of her back, the bulge covered by her loose-fitting rain jacket. Susannah's multiblade Swiss Army knife was tucked in the pocket of her jeans. She'd packed another pocketknife she'd found at Quinn's place in Hunter's backpack, but she'd forgotten to grab it when they stashed the packs. It probably didn't matter—she assumed former First Sergeant Hunter Bragg was probably carrying something even more useful, and deadly. And they both carried small pen-size flashlights, in case they needed to provide their own light.

They entered the hotel through the basement door and stopped just inside a narrow corridor that ended at a simple steel door about ten yards away. "Tell me that door isn't locked," Hunter said quietly.

She had no idea whether it would be, she realized with dismay. She hadn't even remembered there was a second door into the maintenance area. "Only one way to find out." Bracing herself, she strode forward and turned the door handle.

It gave easily, the door swinging open with the faintest of creaks. A shiver of relief washed through her and she edged inside the larger maintenance area.

The mysterious, humming source of the hotel's electricity, air-conditioning and heat wasn't visible from this part of the basement, hidden behind a row of doors that lined the left side of a wider corridor leading from the garage to the service elevators located near the center of the room. Susannah bypassed the elevators and went to a large steel door just beyond. EMERGENCY EXIT was written in bright red letters on a sign just over the doorframe.

The door opened into a roomy stairwell. Once she and Hunter made it inside the relative safety of the enclosed area, Susannah let out a gusty sigh of relief.

"On the service elevators, this is marked *P* for Parking. I think the stairway doors to the floor levels should be marked the same way—lobby will be one, second floor two, etc." She realized he was looking at her with a faint smile on his face. "Oh, right. You worked maintenance here. You probably already knew that."

He shrugged. "I did. And you're right. That's how they're marked. So where do you want to go first?"

"My office," she said. "I want to see if Marcus Lemonde is hiding anything in his desk that we need to know about."

As they reached the lobby level, she reached for the door, but Hunter caught her wrist before she could push the handle. "Let's go up another flight. If I'm remembering the floor plans correctly, this door comes out in view of the lobby desk. We go up to second, we can go down the hall, come back down from the other side and none of the night staff is likely to see us."

"Good thinking," she conceded, following him up one more flight of stairs to the second floor. So far, her healing feet weren't giving her too much trouble, thanks to the excellent fit of the tennis shoes Hunter had purchased at the thrift store and the last-minute bandaging job he'd done before they left Quinn's cabin.

"How're you holding up?" he asked as they opened the door that led into the second-floor corridor.

"I'm good. How's your leg?"

He slanted a narrow-eyed look her way. "It's fine."

Okay, then. Not a profitable topic of conversation.

"It hurts," he said a moment later as they edged out into the hallway after a quick look around. "Some days worse than others. Like I said before, lots of bolts and pins in there."

The hallway was deserted, the lights set on emergency lighting. There had been a few times Susannah had pulled an all-nighter preparing for a big event at the hotel, so she was used to the look of the place after hours.

But apparently Hunter hadn't worked any evening or night shifts during his short stint in the hospitality industry. "Is it always this dark at night?"

"Saves power, which saves money. Because it's occupied, they don't cut out the lights, even in the business section of the hotel. But after six, they go to what they call the evening protocol, cutting out all but essential exit lighting."

"So if we turn on the light in your office, someone's likely to spot it from outside."

"If they're looking."

"I think we have to assume they will be."

Susannah stopped with her hand on the door of the stairwell at the far end of the corridor. "You really think they'll be watching my office?"

"I honestly don't know. I just think we have to go on the assumption that they're watching. Safer that way." He closed his hand over hers, pushing the door to the stairwell open.

She slipped inside, trying to ignore the little shudder of awareness that rippled through her as his body pressed close against her back. He placed his hand over her arm, stilling her forward movement, as the door clicked shut behind them.

In the echo chamber of the stairwell, his whisper sounded impossibly loud. "Speaking of assuming the worst, what if there's already someone in your office when we get there?"

"You mean Marcus?"

"If he's up to his eyes in this plot, he might be here, finalizing things," Hunter said.

"We're armed. We take him down, tie him up and make him tell us what they have planned." She was only half joking, she realized.

Hunter looked at her through narrowed eyes. "Bloodthirsty."

"Just tired of sleeping in strange beds." She

shot him an apologetic glance. "Not that your bed wasn't perfectly nice. And really quite warm." As warm as the air in the stairwell had become since they'd been standing there, pressed intimately close. She edged away from him before she did something reckless, like stand on her tiptoes and kiss him. "There's a window in the door of my office. It's not very large, but it should allow us to take a look inside to see if anyone's moving about."

The first-floor corridor was empty when they eased through the stairwell door into the hall. Handing over the office key, Hunter scouted ahead a few yards, stopping just long enough to glance through the window in the office door. "All clear," he said softly, moving up the hall to make sure they were still alone as she scooted toward her office.

She unlocked the door and slipped into the darkened room, her heart knocking in rapid thuds against her sternum. Crazy, she thought, that two days ago, this office was as familiar and comfortable to her as her own apartment. Now it felt like an alien place, full of shadows and threat.

The door handle rattled behind her, and she whipped around, her hand already closing on the Glock tucked behind her back.

Hunter held up his hands. "I come in peace."

She dropped her hand to her side, squeezing her trembling fingers into a fist. "All quiet?"

He nodded, moving past her to the windows, where the wooden blinds were currently levered open. One by one, he eased the blinds closed, then turned back to look at her. She could barely see him in the faint light seeping in through the window in the door, the dimmed hall lights offering little in the way of illumination.

Pulling his penlight from his pocket, he nodded toward her desk. "The cops have probably already searched your desk—was there anything in there that would reveal your real identity?"

"No," she said firmly.

"Does such a thing exist?" he asked curiously as he flicked on the penlight and aimed the narrow beam on Marcus's desk. "Anywhere?"

"Not anymore." After her grandmother's death, with nothing else to connect her to her old life but a blood vendetta she'd spent over a decade desperate to elude, she'd destroyed the handful of keepsakes she'd held on to for memory's sake.

Her grandmother had never been sentimental, and she'd managed to strip most sentiment from Susannah, as well. There hadn't been a lot to hold on to, anyway. Just memories of a foolish mother, a venal father and a weak brother who could have made a better choice for his life but chose to follow in his father's shiftless footsteps instead.

And her grandmother, who never sat for a photo in her life besides her driver's license photo.

She crossed to where he crouched, looking under Marcus's desk. "I used to have a piece of an old driver's license that belonged to my grandmother. The photo part." It had been one of the keepsakes she'd finally destroyed after her grandmother's death, the grainy photo almost a decade old. Her grandmother had cut up the license when she'd received a new one shortly before the shooting that had sent Susannah out of town.

Hunter looked up at her. "Just the photo part?"

"She'd cut it up when she got her new license in the mail," Susannah explained, tugging at the top right-hand door of the desk. "This is locked."

Hunter pulled a small wallet from his jeans pocket. "I was prepared for that possibility." He flipped open the slim leather wallet to reveal something that brought back a few old, unpleasant memories for Susannah.

"You have a lock-pick kit?"

He glanced at her again. "You know what a lock-pick kit looks like?"

"Did I mention my daddy was a thief?" She watched as he wielded the thin pieces of metal to pop open the lock on the drawer. "Explains why I was living with my grandmother, huh?"

"What happened to the picture of your grandmother?" he asked as his penlight flicked across a collection of perfectly ordinary office-desk minutiae—a small box of staples, a few loose rubber bands, several paper clips in a variety of sizes. Nothing that screamed "domestic terrorist."

"I burned it after she died." The memory stung. "She would have wanted me to. In fact, she'd have been furious if she'd known I'd kept the picture. She was so adamant about changing everything about my life, including my past."

"She was probably right. If the wrong person had seen it—"

"I didn't keep it on me. I bought this old locket at an antique store in Raleigh. A cheap piece of junk jewelry, but I kept my grandmother's driver's-license photo inside that locket. I never wore it or anything. Just kept it around so I could open it when I was feeling lonely."

Hunter put his hand on her arm, his touch gentle and deliciously warm. "I'm sorry you've had to live that way."

"As long as there's a Bradbury in these hills, I'll be living that way. I guess it's time to stop wishing for something else."

Hunter closed his other hand around her arm, penlight and all. "Don't stop wishing for something else. When you stop wishing, you start dying."

"Why does that sound like the voice of experience?" she murmured, her heart hurting a little at the sight of his bleak expression, barely visible in the gloom.

"Because it is." He gave her arms a squeeze and let go, turning back to the desk.

With the lock picks, he unlatched the rest of the drawers. In the top left drawer, the beam of the penlight flickered across what looked like loose tea leaves scattered along the right edge of the drawer.

"Hmm," Susannah said.

"What?"

She waved at the dried leaves. "I never figured Marcus as a tea drinker. In fact, I don't think I've ever seen him drink anything but coffee before."

"Well, I don't think he's going to wipe out a cop conference with a bunch of rogue tea leaves, so maybe we should look elsewhere." Hunter closed the desk drawer and looked around the office. "Is there anything you can remember about Lemonde that might lead you to believe he's not what he seems?"

"Honestly? We don't really interact that much.

He tends to do his job without talking much, which is fine by me."

"Antisocial much?"

She arched an eyebrow. "Pot…kettle…"

He grinned at her retort before his expression grew serious again. "Where would his personnel records be kept?"

"Actually," she said, moving toward the file cabinets behind her desk, "I should have a copy in here somewhere." Flicking on her penlight, she aimed the beam toward the top drawer of the cabinet on the left and pulled it open, grimacing as some dark powder came off on her fingers. "Ugh, is that fingerprint powder?"

Pausing at the edge of her desk, Hunter pulled a couple of tissues from the box by her phone. "Here."

"Thanks." She wiped her fingers on the tissue, then used it to pull the drawer open wider so she could get to the file tucked in the back. She pulled it out and carried it over to her desk. "He had pretty good references from his last job."

"Which was?"

"Public relations at a construction company. The hotel wanted someone who'd worked in the real estate and construction industry because we're interested in bringing in more manufacturing events." She scanned the résumé that sat on top of the other papers in his file. "Hmm."

"What?" Hunter leaned closer, his chest brushing against her shoulder. A flood of heat swamped her, making her light-headed for a second.

She gripped the edge of the desk and pointed her penlight toward the third entry under "Employment" in his résumé. "He worked for Gibraltar Mining."

"As a PR person?"

She shook her head, alarms clanging in her head. "As an explosives expert."

Hunter closed his hand over her arm, his grip painfully tight. Suddenly he was moving, bundling her along in front of him, heading for the door of the small bathroom behind her desk. He pushed her inside and half closed the door behind them. Within a second, he had his Glock out of the ankle holster and in his hand.

"What—" she managed to get out before he pressed his fingers to her lips, silencing her.

Then she heard the rattle of a key in the office door.

Hunter wrapped his arms around her as she started to shiver, his head bending low until his lips just brushed her ear. "Don't make a sound." The words came out on a soft breath.

Outside the bathroom, a light came on, almost

blinding her. Squinting she peered through the narrow gap between the door and the frame and bit back a gasp as she spotted Marcus Lemonde walking slowly across the office.

Heading straight for the bathroom door.

Chapter Thirteen

Susannah's fingers tightened over Hunter's hand and gave a sharp tug, pulling him backward. For a second, he resisted, but she yanked harder and he gave in, backing deeper into the shadows of the bathroom. He heard the faintest of snicks, the tiniest of rattles, and then she was pulling him with her through the narrow doorway of the bathroom closet.

She pulled the door closed behind them, not quite engaging the latch, and even the ambient light from the hallway that had managed to seep into the bathroom disappeared into inky nothingness.

Susannah's breath was warm against the back of his neck, sending animal awareness prickling through his flesh. She kept her death grip on his hand, her fingers flexing and loosening in a frantic rhythm.

He tucked the Glock into his waistband and reached behind him to catch her other hand, bringing both of her arms around his waist until her body pressed flat against his. The heat of her, the rapid thud of her heartbeat against his spine, felt like a tonic, filling his flagging soul with purpose. With confidence and focus.

He could do this. He could handle whatever happened next, because he had to.

She needed him to.

Footsteps clicked on the tile floor of the office bathroom, and the light came on, sending a narrow sliver of illumination through the crack between the door and the frame. Behind Hunter, Susannah pressed her face against his shoulder. He ran his thumbs soothingly over hers, then released her hands and withdrew the Glock from his waistband.

He felt her moving as well, quick, economical movements that made her body brush his in the tight confines of the bathroom closet. Outside in the bathroom, the water came on, and Susannah leaned closer. "I'm armed now, too." He felt her words more than heard them, the faintest whisper of breath in his ear.

Until today, the idea that the sleek, sophisticated businesswoman he'd been following around for the past three weeks would wield anything more lethal than a letter opener had seemed ludicrous.

But he'd seen her loading the borrowed Glock

that afternoon, her movements quick and confident. She knew her way around a weapon. She'd already proved she was tough enough to brave a mountain hike on wounded feet. And she had enough courage to come here tonight, knowing that her life was in danger on multiple levels, because she had inside information that Hunter needed to complete his mission.

She was a far more amazing woman than he'd given her credit for.

Far too amazing for the likes of him.

The water turned off, followed by retreating footsteps. The light in the bathroom extinguished, plunging them once again into darkness.

A moment later, they heard a click. The door to the office closing?

"We should follow him," he whispered. "See why he's here so late."

"We'd be spotted in a heartbeat," she disagreed. "There's nowhere to hide." She caught his arm and gave a tug, turning him toward her. As he started to speak, she stopped him with her mouth, hot and hard against his. Her tongue swept over his, fiercely demanding, and his heart seemed to bolt like a frightened horse, galloping wildly to keep pace with the frantic rhythm of her pulse against his chest.

She released him almost as suddenly as she'd grabbed him, leaving him feeling off balance.

"Thanks," she whispered. "I needed that."

His eyes had adjusted just enough to the ambient light leaking through the door crack to see the flash of her white teeth as she grinned.

Forget amazing, he thought. The woman was bloody magnificent.

Gathering what wits he had left, he edged out of the closet and into the bathroom, leading with the Glock, while Susannah trailed behind him, one hand on his back, tethering them together. They eased out of the bathroom and into the main office, Hunter sweeping his penlight and weapon together across the room, looking for a trap.

There was no one else there.

He clicked off the penlight. "I don't suppose there's an alternate exit from this office. Besides the main door, I mean."

"Not that I know of."

He sighed, considering their options. If Marcus Lemonde had any suspicion at all that someone had broken into the office, he might be waiting outside to ambush them as they left.

"I'm going to risk it," he said, already moving toward the door.

Her hand closed over his arm, her grip strong, stopping him in his tracks. "You, as in, you alone?"

He turned toward her, saw the anger in her eyes and braced himself. "Yes. Me. Alone."

"And I just stay here and wait for the big, brave man to play hero and then come back and rescue me when it's all over?"

"I wouldn't have put it quite that way. But, yeah."

"I realize we only met a day or two ago, so that might explain why you would think that ordering me to stay here like a good little girl is a smart idea. But it's really, really not." She let go of his wrist.

"Two of us will be more conspicuous."

"It's a hotel corridor. Unless you're the size of a spider, there's nowhere to hide." She shook her head. "Look, I know you're a man of action and all that—"

"And all that?"

"But I think we need to stop, take a breath, let the adrenaline settle down and try to figure out what the BRI has planned for tomorrow before we go running around like a couple of headless chickens."

There was a part of him, a barely leashed part of him, that wanted to tell her she didn't know what the hell she was talking about. He might not be wearing the uniform anymore, but he was still a soldier at his core. A man who took action. Who saw the fight and dived right in.

But Susannah was right. This hotel wasn't his home turf, not really. Marcus Lemonde had been working here a lot longer than he had, and if he was a vital part of whatever the BRI had planned for the conference tomorrow, he had all the advantages.

To win this particular battle, he needed to hunker down and figure out where the planned strike would happen and how to stake out high ground so he'd have the advantage once the battle was underway.

He forced himself to relax, to let the spike of adrenaline ease back to a manageable level. "Okay. You're right."

"I'm right?" Her look of surprise was so comical, he couldn't stop a laugh.

"Yeah. There must be a reason Marcus is working late, and I don't think it's last-minute preparations for a great conference this weekend."

"It may be last-minute preparations, all right." She looked around the office. "You know what? We shouldn't stay here to discuss it. He might come back."

"What do you have in mind?" he asked as she crossed to the file cabinets again.

"We're pretty sure it's the conference that's the target, right?" She opened the top file cabinet and used a penlight to see inside, coming back a moment later with a large file folder she'd pulled from the drawer. "This is my backup file on the conference. I print out two copies of every file

I deal with so that we're never without backups. I'm pretty sure Marcus has the master file but I don't think he even knows about this one."

"And what are we going to find in that file?" he asked as she tucked the folder under one arm and started for the office door.

"Hopefully, answers."

THE MINUTE HAND on her watch clicked past twelve. Two in the morning. They'd been holed up in one of the basement-level maintenance rooms for over an hour, poring over every file, every scrap of paper, every hastily jotted note that Susannah had filed away over the past few months in preparation for the Tri-State Law Enforcement Society's annual conference.

"I keep going back to Marcus's experience with explosives," she said, stifling a yawn as she looked up from yet another voucher. "If the BRI wanted to make a big splash, blowing up that conference would be one way to do it."

"It wouldn't be easy to get their hands on the amount of explosives necessary to make a really big splash," Hunter disagreed. "Anything really high-grade is very hard to procure. That's why people go for things like ANFO—ammonium nitrate and fuel oil."

"I know what ANFO is."

He slanted a look at her. "I'm trying very hard not to ask why you do."

She flashed him a grin. "I'm from the hills, remember? We know how to explode all sorts of things around here."

"Well, it takes a pretty big stash of ANFO or something like it to blow up a big building the size of this hotel. Or even a big section of it. At the Murrah Building in Oklahoma City, they had barrels of the stuff to do the kind of damage that bomb did."

"Maybe they're not going for anything quite that big."

"Billy Dawson seemed pretty sure what he had planned would rival Oklahoma City in scope." He looked down at the file folder on the worktable in front of him, one hand flexing over his left knee. "I was really, really hoping it wasn't going to be explosives, though."

Of course, she thought. The last thing he'd want to deal with would be another explosion.

"Hunter—"

His gaze snapped up to meet hers. "Don't do that."

"Do what?"

"Don't pity me."

She *had* pitied him, once. Before she'd seen his scars and realized just how close he must have been to death after the explosion—and how far he'd come in such a short time.

Pity was the last thing she felt for him.

"I wouldn't dare." She touched his arm. "I just wondered if you think we should call in reinforcements now, while there's still time."

"You mean call Quinn."

"We have nothing to offer the police in the way of evidence, but maybe Quinn has some ideas."

"If he did, he'd have given them to us."

Susannah wasn't so sure. She hadn't spent much time with Alexander Quinn before he'd left them alone in his cabin, but what interaction they'd shared convinced her he was the sort of man who always had an agenda. Did he want them to find out what was going on here at the Highland Hotel and Resort? Absolutely. Did he want them to put a stop to it? She thought so.

But there was a reason he'd assigned Hunter Bragg to this particular job, and Susannah was beginning to suspect Quinn's motives were more about getting something from Bragg than stopping the threat to the conference. Or, at the very least, the two goals were of equal importance to Quinn.

But what was it that he wanted from Hunter?

"Why did Quinn assign this job to you?" she asked as he bent his head back over the hotel floor plans once again, his brow furrowed as he looked for something, anything, they hadn't yet discovered.

"I was a disgruntled vet with a chip on my shoulder," he said with a grimace, his gaze not moving from the floor plans. "Prime militia bait."

"Disgruntled?"

He sighed and turned to look at her. "Not about combat. I mean, yeah, I supposed I'm as frustrated as the next grunt about how wars are all about politics these days, but I'm not out to blow up the Pentagon."

"You just wanted the BRI to think so."

He nodded. "I've been pretty angry since I got back stateside. About this." He pressed the heel of his hand against his bad leg. "About what happened to my sister because of me. At myself for letting it happen."

"You didn't let it happen."

"You don't know that. You weren't there."

"So tell me. What happened?"

He lowered his head. "Let's just concentrate on the job at hand."

"We've been staring at these files for an hour as if we could magically conjure up the answer if we just looked hard enough. My eyes are starting to cross. Let's take a break for a minute." She touched his arm, felt his skin ripple beneath her touch. "I won't ask any more questions if you don't want me to."

His lips flattened to a thin line. "Good."

Silence fell between them, marred only by the soft sounds of their breathing and the hum of the hotel's power plant close by. The small maintenance break room where they'd holed up to do their research was almost as small as her office bathroom, or felt that way, at least, with the large square table in the middle of the cramped space and the long countertop nearby, holding a coffee-maker and a couple of big cans of ground coffee. A tiny refrigerator stood in the corner, its soft hum of electricity swallowed by the noise from the hotel's heating system.

Hardly a place conducive to figuring out how to save the world. Or, for that matter, to save the Tri-State Law Enforcement Society's annual conference from going up in smoke.

Frustration boiling in her gut, she pushed her chair back with a scrape and started to rise, but Hunter grabbed her arm, holding her in place.

"I woke up in the middle of the night and couldn't move. At first, I thought it was a nightmare. I'd been having my share of those." He passed his hand over his jaw, his palm making a whispery sound as it rasped against the beginning of beard stubble. "Then I realized there were hands holding me down. On my legs and my arms. On my head. However they'd gotten into my sister's place, they'd done it without waking me up."

"Where was your sister?"

"She'd gone to a concert in Knoxville with a couple of women from the prosecutor's office. That's where she worked at the time. They made a night of it, booked a room in a hotel near the concert venue." He shook his head. "I don't know how they knew she'd be gone. Or maybe they didn't know. Maybe the plan had been to take me and terrorize her at the same time."

"I know you must have fought back."

His eyes narrowed, his gaze unfocused, as if watching the past play out in his mind. "I think I did. I think I must have. They put something on my face—a cloth drenched in something. Maybe chloroform, maybe something else. All I know is, my mind went to a complete fog and the next time I could think clearly, I was cuffed to a water pipe in a cabin in the middle of nowhere. And there I stayed until the cops showed up to rescue me. Way too late to be any help to Janet."

"You think that constitutes letting it happen to you?"

He grimaced as if in pain. "I should have figured out something. Gotten loose somehow. Or, hell, if I hadn't gotten myself blown up in Afghanistan—"

"I suppose that was your fault, too?" She couldn't quite keep the dry sarcasm out of her voice.

He snapped his gaze up to hers, his eyes blazing with anger. "Getting blown up might not have been my fault, but—"

When he didn't continue, she looked down at his leg, watching his fingers as they massaged his thigh. "But something was?"

His lips parted and a shaky breath escaped his lips. His fingers clenched around his leg, so tightly that she knew it must hurt.

She released a gusty little sigh. "Forget it. I shouldn't push—"

His gaze locked with hers, raw-eyed and fierce. "It was an early morning patrol, about two years ago. Helmand Province. Predawn."

She eased back into her chair, her heart pounding. She'd wanted details, but now that he was talking, her chest tightened with dread.

"We weren't really fighting anymore by then. Just trying to keep a lid on the tension. Taliban, warlords battling it out for turf in the opium trade—wild, wild West kind of stuff. If we weren't there, they'd have been happy enough to slaughter each other. But we gave them a target they could all agree on." His hand slid away from her arm, but she caught it in hers, needing the connection.

His gaze tangled with hers for a moment before he looked away. But he held on to her hand, his grip tightening.

"It was October, and the summer heat had finally passed. The whole place seemed like a dust bowl to us most of the time, so I can't really call it beautiful, but the milder weather had us all feeling like we could breathe again." A smile flirted with his lips but didn't linger. It never touched his haunted eyes. "Maybe we dropped our guard. I don't know. I've been over and over that morning, trying to figure out how we let ourselves get surrounded."

She frowned. "Surrounded?"

He bumped gazes with her again before looking away, his eyes angled forward, toward the blank wall across from them, as if he were watching something playing out on the flat surface, something she couldn't picture. Didn't want to picture.

"Sometimes that was the point of the IEDs," he said softly. "To make the troops vulnerable to attack. Blow up the vehicle and prey on the survivors."

Susannah's gut roiled. "Did they—"

"Prey on me?" His mouth twisted in a gro-

Paula Graves   221

tesque parody of a smile. "No, not me. I was lucky. The blast sent me flying into a small ravine. They didn't know I was there, so they didn't—"

Her fingers flexed, tightening on his.

He turned to look at her again, his gaze holding this time. "This isn't something anyone needs to hear."

"But maybe it's something you need to say."

His gaze held hers a moment longer, then he closed his eyes and leaned toward her until his forehead rested against hers. "I could hear them attacking—" He swallowed hard, his breath releasing in a soft, guttural growl as he pulled away from her. "I could hear them brutalizing the handful of survivors. I could hear it, but I couldn't drag myself up that ravine to lay down any cover fire for them. I've gone over it and over it a million times since that day—if I'd tried a little harder, could I have made it up that rock wall? My leg was a mess, yes, but only one leg. Not the rest of me. Why couldn't I make it up that wall?"

"Stop," she said, fighting a surge of anger as she reached up and cradled his face between her palms, making him look at her. "You nearly lost your leg. You were probably losing blood by the buckets, right? You think you could have saved anyone even if you'd gotten up that wall?"

"I don't know." He lifted his hands, covering hers, pulling her hands away from his face. But he didn't let them go. "I don't know. I just know I wasn't any kind of war hero for being the sole survivor."

She didn't agree. She thought he was a hero just for putting his life on the line there in the first place. But that wasn't what he needed to hear, so she swallowed her protest and simply squeezed his hands. "I'm sorry. I'm sorry it happened to you and your team. I'm sorry they didn't survive."

"Me, too." He released her hands and picked up the folder she'd brought with them. "There's got to be something in here that tells us what they're up to. Some vulnerability we're missing."

"I don't think it's a bomb." She forced her voice past the lump in her throat. "I've looked over and over these floor plans, and I don't see how they could plant a bomb close enough to the conference rooms that would do the damage they're looking to inflict, do you? The best bet would be to pack a large truck or something similar with ANFO or another kind of explosive and set it off with a timer, but there's nowhere to park anything at all on the side of the hotel where the conference is taking place. Those rooms were built specifically for the view of the mountains out the picture windows, and they overlook a bluff. There's no parking area on that side of the building. And unless they were able to set explosives that would bring the whole structure down, like a controlled demolition—"

"We've already looked around for something like that. It's just not here," he said.

"So how else would you try to do damage at a conference if you couldn't blow it up?"

"Radiation poisoning," he suggested.

"God forbid."

"I think we can rule out any sort of armed ambush," he said thoughtfully. He still looked haunted, but some of the tension in his shoulders and neck eased as he applied his mind to their current problem, leaving the past behind. "Assuming the hotel is allowing all those cops to carry weapons. Are they?"

"There was some debate on the topic," she admitted, "but I convinced the naysayers that you can't expect a bunch of cops to agree to hand over their weapons just because they're at a conference."

"So, no armed siege. No bomb. Probably not a suitcase nuke."

She shuddered at the thought. "Unless someone worked down at Oak Ridge and could get their hands on—"

"Not going to happen. Suitcase nukes are more fiction than fact, and if anyone ever successfully pulled it off, the fissile materials would almost certainly come from somewhere overseas." His brow furrowed. "I wonder, though…"

"You wonder?" she prodded when he didn't say anything more.

"I was thinking about the rash of polonium poisonings in Europe a while back. Remember those?"

"Vaguely. Didn't everybody think that the current incarnation of what used to be the KGB did it? Eliminating enemies of the state or something?"

"Or something," he agreed. "And polonium wouldn't be easy to get your hands on, especially for the BRI. But poisoning a food source isn't that hard if you have access to the catering kitchen. All kinds of ways to do it, I'd think. Who's catering the deal?"

"Ballard's," she answered. "It's a large catering outfit in Maryville." Her stomach dropped. "Oh, my God. Of course."

"What?"

"Marcus is the one who hired them. He'd been handling the whole thing until about three weeks ago, when I found out he was dating one of the chefs. I couldn't exactly change caterers so close to the event, but I did relieve him of his liaison duties and took them over myself. I didn't want there to be any whiff of a conflict of interest."

"Three weeks ago is when Billy Dawson called me and the others in to discuss ways to get you out of the way." He reached across the space between them and brushed her hair away from her temple, letting his fingertips linger on her cheek. "They're going to poison the conference luncheon."

Chapter Fourteen

"The caterer is bringing their own cooking pans and utensils, but they'll be using the conference-hall kitchen." Susannah was pacing the small break room in agitated strides, circling the table where Hunter sat as she spoke. "The conference dining hall is on the second floor."

"I know."

"The kitchen is just off the main hall," she added as if he hadn't spoken. Her gaze was angled forward, but he knew she wasn't really seeing the drab break-room walls, with the out-of-date wall calendar displaying Miss August in tight jeans and a crop top, wrench in one hand and toolbox in the other. Instead, he knew, she was picturing the second-floor layout, from the large banquet hall in the center to the compact kitchen in the next suite over.

"Do they police access to the kitchens?"

She looked at him that time, her gaze shifting into focus. "Not really. Not unless we're asked to."

"Did the top cops ask you to?"

"No."

"Okay." He reached out and caught her hand as she wandered past, pulling her off course. She almost stumbled into his lap before catching herself with one hand on his shoulder.

Her gaze darkened as he dropped his other hand to the curve of her hip, holding her in place. "Do you know anything about poisons?"

She shook her head. "Nothing that didn't come from true-crime TV."

"I don't know much, myself," he admitted, leaving his hand in place. He liked the soft heat of her body beneath his fingers, liked the way the sensation spread up his arm and into his chest like a river of warmth. "My expertise tends to be chemical weapons, thanks to my training."

"I don't think it can be anything fast-acting," she said thoughtfully. She seemed to be leaning into his touch, so he let go of her wrist and laid his hand on her other hip, gently drawing her closer. She took a couple of steps forward, settling between his knees. She wrapped one hand around the back of his neck, her other hand toying with the collar of his shirt. "If it was fast, someone would figure it out before everyone was affected. So what poisons would that eliminate? Cyanide?"

"Cyanide's definitely fast-acting." He leaned

toward her, drawn by the heat of her body. So tempting and comforting at the same time. "What's the menu?"

"The usual. Mixed-green salad. Baked chicken and asparagus in a cream sauce for meat-eaters, and grilled portabello mushrooms with wild rice and asparagus in a basil sauce for vegetarians."

"Poisonous mushrooms?"

"I don't know. The caterers are supplying all the main ingredients. I'm wondering if it's something that has to be added here rather than at the caterer's. Since Marcus is here so late. Maybe he's switching out something the caterers brought early, like condiments or something that doesn't have to be brought here fresh?"

"Maybe herbs or spices?"

"Oh, my God," she said, remembering the leaves they'd seen in Marcus's desk drawer. "What if those weren't tea leaves in his desk?"

"I think we'd better figure out a way into that kitchen."

"SHE'S SOMEWHERE INSIDE that hotel." Kenny Bradbury's voice had risen a half octave since Asa's arrival, his dark brown eyes glowing with a chaotic mix of excitement and anxiety.

"You're absolutely sure?"

"We had a rifle scope camera on the office

windows, like you suggested. How'd you know she'd go back there?"

Because that was the kind of girl Susan McKenzie had always been, even at sixteen. A tough little hillbilly girl who never gave up on a fight.

He knew that the Blue Ridge Infantry was up to something at the hotel. He wasn't a member himself, but in his business, it was impossible to avoid rubbing elbows with people who were part of that ridiculous mock army. Not the sort of people he could trust with his business, of course, but they were sometimes useful as informants or, occasionally, cannon fodder.

"Did you get a shot of her?" Asa asked Kenny.

Kenny pulled out the rifle scope camera and showed him the image on the display. The lighting wasn't great—she and the man with her were using small, low-power flashlights, and the narrow beams barely provided enough light to make out their features.

But the shape of the face was right. The slight upward curve of her nose. Those full lips that Clinton had been downright obsessed with, obsessed enough to risk everything to have her, even though she didn't want any part of him.

Stupid fool.

"It's definitely her, right?" Kenny asked, his

earlier confidence beginning to flag in the wake of Asa's continued silence.

He sighed and let his cousin off the hook. "It's her. You have the exits covered so she can't get away?"

"Every one of them."

Asa made a note to confirm that fact for himself. It had been years since he'd been anywhere near this close to finding little Susan McKenzie and bringing her to justice.

It was way past time to get the whole mess over with.

"THERE'S A DUMBWAITER," Susannah said suddenly, tapping her fingers on the piece of paper in front of her with a jolt of excitement.

Hunter leaned toward her to look at the paper, his hard-muscled shoulder pressed to hers, distracting tingles racing along her flesh where they touched. "Where?"

"In the conference-room kitchen." She pointed to the notation on a copy of the security department's correspondence with the caterer. "The caterer asked if we had parking-level access to the conference-room kitchen by way of a dumbwaiter, and security says yes."

"It's not on the floor plans."

"Maybe it was added after the plans were drawn." She reached for the hotel floor plans, locating the conference-room kitchen. "Okay, the kitchen is about twenty yards east of the central elevators." She rose and walked to the break-room door, edged her head out the door and looked toward the elevators. "All clear. Shall we go hunting?"

Hunter stayed close as they crossed to the central bank of elevators and looked east. About twenty yards down the narrow hallway was a door located close to the exit that led to the parking garage. "That must be it," he said. "It's the room where the main breaker and fuse boxes are. I'm not sure I've ever actually been in there."

"Me, either." They tried the door, found it locked. Hunter pulled out the keys he'd grabbed from the maintenance office and unlocked the door.

The room was larger than he'd expected, covered nearly wall to wall with a variety of electrical boxes and numerous switches and levers. "Careful," he warned as she moved past him into the room, toward the only place the dumbwaiter could possibly be located: a narrow door in the wall between the main breaker and a small gray fuse box.

"Please be unlocked," she murmured as she twisted the doorknob.

The door opened with ease, revealing what looked like a small closet with a square metal cage filling most of the upper half of the space.

A sturdy cable hung on a pulley to one side of the dumbwaiter.

"Bingo," Susannah murmured, flashing him a grin.

"It's too small for me," he said, his voice dark with frustration.

"But not for me."

His gaze clashed with hers. "No, Susannah."

"Yes, Hunter."

"We came here together, and I plan for us to leave together. And the only way to ensure that is if we stay together."

"We need to get into the kitchen. There are only two ways for that to happen—either I take that elevator up to the second floor and risk being seen in the hallway, or I sneak into the kitchen in this dumbwaiter. I know which option I'd rather choose."

"What if you get up there and Marcus Lemonde is waiting on the other side?"

"I'm armed."

"He may be, too."

"I'm not afraid of Marcus." She'd faced down much tougher enemies. "Look, I know you're only trying to protect me. But I'm not helpless. When I was sixteen, I killed a man trying to rape me. And then I left home a few weeks later after that man's family tried to kill me in retaliation. I've lived isolated from everything and everyone who ever meant a damn thing to me because that's the only way I knew to survive. Now, I have a chance to stop an attack on a group of people who are out there, day in and day out, trying to keep people like you and me safe from harm."

"Susannah—"

"Susan," she snapped. "My name is Susan. Susan Elizabeth McKenzie. I'll probably never get to use it again, but I just want one person to know who I really am."

Hunter touched her cheek, his thumb sliding over her trembling bottom lip. "Nice to meet you, Susan Elizabeth McKenzie."

"One of the people who'll be eating at that conference luncheon is my cousin, whose family took me in when I had literally nowhere else to turn." She pulled away from his grasp, afraid she couldn't stay strong while he was touching her. "I have to find out what the BRI has planned for the conference. And I have to put a stop to it."

Tension crackled between them in the thick silence. Then Hunter gave a short, barely-there nod and looked away from her.

"What are the odds that this thing doesn't creak like a rusty hinge?" Wincing in anticipation, she climbed into the steel cage. There was a faint rasp of metal on metal, but the dumbwaiter seemed sturdy enough.

"You don't have to do this." Hunter's voice

was a growly whisper. He didn't meet her eyes, his gaze focused on the rope-and-pulley system designed to move the dumbwaiter up and down the chute between floors. "We can figure out another option."

"We could be running out of time," she replied, reaching across the space between them to curl her fingers over his arm.

He looked at her then, his green eyes blazing a maelstrom of emotions her way. Anger was there. Fear. And something else, something that rang through her like a newly struck bell, true and resonant.

"When you reach the top, tug three times on the rope to let me know you're there and you're okay. And be careful. Don't take chances you don't have to." He bent in a rush, slanting his mouth over hers in a fierce kiss. His lips softened within a second, caressing hers with such tenderness she felt her heart contract.

He pulled away as quickly as he'd moved toward her, reaching for the rope. He gave a tug, the pulley turned and the dumbwaiter began to rise.

She hadn't counted on the darkness. Once she was inside the chute, the dumbwaiter blocked out almost all light from above or below, plunging her into a lurching void of darkness and jerky motion. Steeling herself against a rush of panic, she concentrated on breathing in slow, steady rhythm with the pulse in her ears. One breath for every four heartbeats. In and out.

With a jarring clunk, the dumbwaiter jolted to a stop. Playing her penlight on the surface in front of her, she saw she had reached another door.

She tugged three times on the rope, knowing Hunter would be able to feel the vibrations on his end. Then, holding her breath and lifting a quick, fervent prayer, she opened the door.

Beyond was more darkness.

SOLDIERS WERE NO bloody good at waiting. They were men and women of action. The point of the spear. Hunter felt useless standing there holding a dumbwaiter rope and waiting for someone else to take all the risks.

When his cell phone vibrated against his chest, it felt as jolting as a bolt of electricity. He shoved his hand into the jacket's inside chest pocket and withdrew his phone. An unfamiliar number on the display threw him for a second, until he remembered Quinn had a new burner phone.

He answered with the "all clear" code phrase Quinn had given him at the cabin before he left. "Baker Electric twenty-four-hour hotline."

"My garbage disposal has a short," Quinn answered.

Hunter relaxed marginally at the sound of the "situation normal" response code.

"Anything new?" Quinn asked after a brief pause.

"We have an idea how the BRI plans to target the conference." Hunter told Quinn about Marcus Lemonde's connection to the catering company and their theory about how he planned to sabotage the luncheon. "Depending on what kind of poison they go with, the results could range from mild sickness to mass murder."

"You've been inside the BRI for three months," Quinn said. "What's your gut feeling? How far are they willing to go?"

"At one point, I thought they might be blowing this place up," he answered grimly. "I don't think they'd balk at mass murder."

"The question is, do they have a bigger agenda?" Quinn fell silent on his end of the line for a few seconds, causing Hunter to wonder if he'd lost the phone connection. But a second later, Quinn added, "What are you doing now?"

"Holding a rope," Hunter answered, not hiding his frustration.

THE DARK SPACE beyond the door turned out to be the conference-room kitchen, as they'd hoped. Painting the dark space with the narrow beam of the penlight, Susannah mapped the long narrow room in her mind, then shut off the small light and navigated in the darkness.

There was a large, stainless-steel refrigerator in one corner. She eased the door open, the automatic light inside the refrigerator casting a glow across the immediate area. It gave her enough illumination to make out the rest of the long, narrow room—large commercial cooking ranges, double ovens, a pair of high-powered microwave ovens and what looked to be a large double-door pantry barely visible from this end of the kitchen.

After a quick look in the refrigerator revealed it to be empty, she closed the door and flicked her penlight on again, crossing to take a look inside the pantry.

Unlike the refrigerator, the pantry seemed to be stocked with basic cooking staples. Cans of chicken, beef and vegetable broth sat on one shelf, along with canned evaporated milk and several cans of tomato paste. Standard herbs and spices took up space on the shelf below. The bottom two shelves were occupied by flour, sugar and cornmeal in carefully labeled canisters.

Susannah scanned the pantry contents again, trying to think logically. The canned items seemed to be unlikely potential sources of a poisoning, sealed as they were. The spices might be better bets, but it would probably take a lab days to work out what the ingredients of those bottles really were.

Being quick about it, she looked into the canisters and confirmed that the contents did seem to be sugar, flour and cornmeal. There was also a large cylindrical carton of basic table salt and, near that, three pepper mills containing three different colors of peppercorns.

In other words, she was looking at a fairly standard kitchen pantry. With any number of herbs and spices that might look like those leaves in Marcus's desk.

If those leaves had anything to do with the plot at all.

Focus. If Marcus wanted to poison the food, how would he go about it?

Marcus was dating the woman from the catering company, but removing him from acting as a liaison with the caterer had seemed to be a sufficient change to waylay any possible questions of ethics.

Little had she known just how bloody unethical Marcus Lemonde could be when he put his mind to it.

Based on her discussions with the catering company, and the notes she'd made in her files, Ballard's Catering was supplying all of the primary ingredients for the dishes they were preparing, but they had asked for the hotel to supply the cooking facility and basic staples. Susannah imagined they'd probably include salt and pepper as basic staples. What about other herbs? Could Marcus have tainted the herbs in the pantry in some way? Maybe with those leaves they'd found in his desk?

She looked over the possibilities. If those leaves were a plant poison, such as belladonna or maybe hemlock, he could pretty easily mix them into aromatics like oregano or basil, couldn't he? She grabbed those spice bottles as well as the ground thyme and the small bottle of bay leaves. Maybe Alexander Quinn could test these herbs for toxins before the conference started tomorrow—

As she turned away from the pantry shelves, she heard a quiet click, followed by a slow, steady cadence of tapping, moving inexorably closer. Footsteps, she realized, shoving down a sudden spike of panic.

Padding across the narrow kitchen floor as quietly as possible, she hurried back to the dumbwaiter and folded herself inside, wincing as the heel of one foot caught the edge of the steel cage, making a soft thunking noise. Closing the door behind her, she gave the pulley rope four sharp tugs. The dumbwaiter lurched briefly and began a shuddering descent.

It was making too much noise, she thought,

her heart rate climbing until her pulse seemed to hammer in her head like a piston.

Suddenly, the dumbwaiter seemed to drop precipitously, stopping with a loud clang that made her teeth crack together. It didn't move again.

"Hunter?" Keeping her voice to a whisper, she extended her hand in the dark, expecting to find the cool steel of the dumbwaiter chute. Instead, she felt solid wood.

It was the door in the basement. But why wasn't it open?

"Hunter?" she whispered again, sliding her hand to the right in search of the doorknob.

There. She gave it a turn, suddenly terrified she would find it locked, trapping her in the dark. But the knob turned easily enough, and she shoved the door open, already halfway out of the dumbwaiter by the time she realized it wasn't Hunter standing on the other side of the door.

"Hello, Susan. Nice to see you again after such a long time."

Ice flooding her veins, Susannah stared into the feral smile of Asa Bradbury.

Chapter Fifteen

Hunter had never lost consciousness, only the ability to move with any coordination until the thumping pain in his head subsided to a dull throb. But those few seconds had been enough time for the four men who'd ambushed him to strip away his Glock and the folding knife he kept in his jeans pocket.

Unarmed and outnumbered, he had few options. Better to let them think he was unconscious. It wasn't as if he'd be able to do much to thwart them with his head pounding and his limbs currently feeling like wet noodles.

But he had to keep his mind alert. Because whoever these guys were, they weren't Billy Dawson's BRI thugs. Which meant—

He heard the door of the dumbwaiter open, the scrambling sound of someone—Susannah—crawling out. Her footsteps faltered, and for a second, the whole room seemed to grow utterly still.

Then one of the men who'd wrestled him to

the floor spoke in a hill country drawl. "Hello, Susan. Nice to see you again after such a long time."

Panic clawed at Hunter's gut, clanged along his nerves and pushed through the misty half fog in his brain. Lying perfectly still while his mind was whirling like a tornado took every ounce of control he had.

"Asa Bradbury." Susannah's voice was low and remarkably calm, considering she was apparently facing the man who'd driven her into exile nearly a decade ago. "It saddens me to see you here. I really thought you were the rare Bradbury who had a lick of sense."

"I'm chock-full of sense, sugar." From the tone of the man's voice, Hunter suspected he was smiling. "Primarily a sense of justice."

"Justice. Really."

The man she'd called Asa sighed. "You killed a kinsman, Susie. You know it's not something a Bradbury can just let go."

"Even though your kinsman was trying to rape a sixteen-year-old girl in her own bedroom?"

"Sadly, even then."

"And so, what? Summary execution? Shall we just get it over with right here and now?"

Hunter's pulse stuttered in his ears, escalating the ache in his head. He sneaked a look at the scene through his eyelashes, taking in the four men circling Susannah, guns drawn. Her gaze slanted toward him, and for an electric second, he thought she could see through his ruse.

But she looked back at the tallest of the four men, the one she'd called Asa. "What's it going to be, Asa?"

"There will be a tribunal tomorrow morning at ten. Your crimes against our family will be aired, and you can defend yourself." Asa Bradbury's tone was almost formal, as if he really did believe he was behaving according to some code of honor, however twisted.

"And if my defense is found wanting?" Her voice was deep and raspy.

"An eye for an eye," Asa answered. He nodded his head toward the others, and they moved even closer to Susannah.

"Wait," she said, her gaze slanting toward Hunter again. He closed his eyes, in case anyone followed her gaze. "Is he—"

"He's alive. He isn't our concern."

"What did you do to him?"

"Incapacitated him so that he couldn't try to keep us from doing what we came here to do." Asa's tone was dismissive, as if Hunter was no more significant to him than a door that had had to be unlocked to reach Susannah.

"I have to leave something for him," Susannah said.

Hunter heard the shuffle of feet and risked a quick peek through his eyelashes. She was trying to move past the three men who'd surrounded her, but they held her in place. "Please, Asa. I get that you're going to take me out of here no matter what I have to say about it, but we were trying to stop a mass murder from taking place. That's why he and I are here."

Asa glanced toward Hunter, forcing him to close his eyes again. "Also not our concern."

"I never realized you were a monster, Asa."

"I'm not."

"Then let me give him these."

Hunter heard more shuffling noises, but he didn't dare open his eyes.

"What are these?" Asa asked.

"Herbs. We think someone's planning to poison people at a conference tomorrow, and Hunter will need to get these herbs tested. Time is essential. Please let me leave these for him."

For a long moment, there was no sound at all beyond the soft whisper of breathing. Then Hunter heard footsteps moving toward him. Heavy footsteps, so definitely not Susannah's. He heard the soft click of something hard thudding against the floor near his head.

"I need to leave a note," Susannah said, her voice still a few feet away.

"Unnecessary. I'm sure your friend will figure

it out." Asa's voice moved away from Hunter as the man joined his companions where they held Susannah captive. "It's time for us to go."

"I don't know why you pretend this is going to be justice, Asa," Susannah said as he and the other three men pushed her toward the exit door. "There's nobody on Laurel Bald who'll choose my word over yours. You know that. Why not just get this over with here and now?"

What was she doing, trying to goad them into killing her right now? Had she lost her mind?

Then, as the door closed behind them, he realized what she'd said.

Laurel Bald.

Brilliant, beautiful woman. She'd just given him somewhere to start looking for her.

HE'D BEEN CONSCIOUS, hadn't he? All Susannah had seen was the slightest flicker of his eyelids, but there had been a tension in his stillness that convinced her Hunter had been conscious, at least for the last few minutes of her confrontation with the Bradburys.

But had he picked up on the clue she'd given him?

"I know you think this is unfair." Beside her, Asa Bradbury shifted in his seat, the movement tugging the handcuffs that chained her to Asa's wrist.

"How on earth did you figure that out?" she responded in a tone as dry as desert sand.

"Do you think I'm unaware of my brother's more venal pursuits?" Asa asked softly, his head turned to look at her.

She made herself meet his gaze, unsurprised to find a hint of sympathy in the man's dark eyes. She hadn't been lying when she'd said she'd always thought Asa had more sense than most of the Bradburys. He hadn't been part of the family's meth business, at least not back when she'd still been living in Boneyard Ridge.

But she supposed things might have changed.

"Our family is in a battle for its life," Asa added more quietly. He sounded genuinely regretful, and Susannah supposed he might be, at that. Being the titular head of a mountain crime family had to be stressful for a man like Asa, who'd once dreamed about leaving the mountains to see the world outside. He'd wanted to go to college, maybe come back with a business degree and the chance to build a different sort of reputation for the Bradbury name.

But most of the other Bradburys had liked their name just the way it was. Synonymous with brute power and fast, dirty money.

"What happened to you, Asa?" she asked softly. "You had such plans for your life."

He didn't answer, but the tense set of his profile suggested she'd found a sore spot.

"You could let me go. Just end this madness here, once and for all. You know I didn't do anything that wasn't my God-given right. I had a right to protect myself from Clinton. I had a right to choose what to do with my own body."

"I can't stop them," he said quietly. "I can barely control them as it is, and if I were to show any sign of softness—"

"They'd destroy you," she finished for him, overwhelmed with hopelessness.

"I *am* sorry." Asa looked at her then, his brown eyes surprisingly sympathetic. "I always liked you, Susie McKenzie. You had fire."

She looked away, her gaze settling on the back of Kenny Bradbury's shaggy head where he sat in the driver's seat of the panel van carrying her inexorably toward her fate.

Please, she thought, *please let Hunter have been conscious. Please let him figure out what I was trying to tell him.*

"THESE NEED TO be tested for toxins," Hunter said without preamble, handing Alexander Quinn the four bottles of herbs Susannah had taken from the hotel kitchen before she'd been ambushed by the Bradburys. Quinn had met him on the road at the place where Hunter and Susannah had stashed their extra supplies. "And if there's anything in them, the cops need to get a warrant for Marcus Lemonde's desk in the Event Planning office."

Hunter bent to pick up both packs and slung them over one shoulder, already headed back to the borrowed SUV.

Quinn followed at a brisk pace. "Where are you going?"

"Boneyard Ridge. There's a place there called Laurel Bald. That's where they're taking her."

"The Bradburys?" Quinn asked.

Hunter stopped midstep, turning to look at his boss. "You knew about the Bradburys?" All he'd told Quinn on the phone was that their plans had gone sideways and now Susannah had been kidnapped. He hadn't mentioned the Bradburys. Of that, he was certain.

"I know her real name is Susan McKenzie and that she killed a man named Clinton Bradbury when she was sixteen years old."

Hunter stared at Quinn in silence before he breathed out a stream of profanities. "Of course you knew. You know every damn thing there is to know about everybody, don't you? You probably even knew that if you assigned me to watch her, I'd end up willing to take a bullet for her. Because I'm that sort of guy, aren't I?"

"Yes, you are. I just didn't have any idea you'd

be willing to do it because you'd fallen in love with her."

Hunter started to protest, but the words never got past the back of his throat. What was the point of arguing? If he wasn't already in love with her, he was awfully close, wasn't he? Even now, the thought that he might not reach her in time to stop the Bradburys from doing whatever they planned to do to her was enough to make him feel weak-kneed and sick.

But it was also enough to make him ignore the pain still throbbing in his head, because he didn't have time to worry about whether or not he had a concussion. He couldn't afford to wait for a CAT scan or to get checked out by the paramedics.

Susannah needed him. And she'd given him a way to find her.

"You're going after her." It wasn't a question.

"I am," Hunter said, already moving toward the SUV again.

"You'll need backup."

"I probably will," he conceded, opening the driver's-side door.

"I'll get these samples to a lab. And I'll put some agents on call. Will six be enough? They can be in Boneyard Ridge in half an hour. Siege protocol?"

Hunter thought about it. He wasn't sure how many Bradburys there were in Boneyard Ridge, but unless they were all commando-trained warriors, they wouldn't be any match for seven well-trained agents from The Gates.

"Six should do it. Siege protocol," he agreed as he slid behind the steering wheel and put the keys in the ignition. "If there aren't toxins in those herbs, then get back to that hotel and figure out what Billy Dawson's up to, even if you have to call in a fake bomb threat to get the cops involved. Because I've got something else to do."

Hunter put the SUV in Drive and pulled away from Quinn, heading north toward Boneyard Ridge.

DAWN WAS STILL several hours away when the panel van carrying Susannah and her captors chugged its way up the winding mountain road to Laurel Bald near the top of Boneyard Ridge. Next to her, Asa Bradbury released an audible sigh, as if reaching his home territory came as a physical relief.

She herself felt nothing but sheer, gut-twisting panic. No matter how much she'd once loved this place, Boneyard Ridge had long since become a place of fear and loathing. Her grandmother was gone from this place, leaving only a mixed bag of memories and the ever-present threat of violence and retribution.

Retribution she was about to face, after so many years trying to run from the inevitable.

"Where do you plan to keep me?" she asked, trying not to let her fear show.

She could tell from the look in Asa's eyes that she hadn't been successful. "Jennalyn's cabin. She's made you up a place to rest in the cellar. It'll be a mite cold, so I asked her to make sure you had extra blankets."

"You're keeping me prisoner in a root cellar. In October."

"Did you expect a comfortable guest suite?" he asked in a flat tone, slanting another look her way. "You killed my brother."

"In self-defense."

"So you say."

"You know it was self-defense. You as much as admitted it."

"You'll have your say at the tribunal."

"Will I be provided with legal counsel?" she countered, deciding to play the game by Asa's rules. If he wanted to pretend he was seeking justice, then she would humor him. But on her own terms.

"You can serve as your own counsel, just as we'll serve as Clinton's."

"And the judge?"

"Three of our elders."

"Names?"

He was silent for a long moment. "Colton Bradbury, Mary Partlain and Brantley Bradbury."

She tried to place their positions in the Bradbury family. Asa's parents were both dead, but Asa's father had had two brothers, if she remembered correctly. "Colton's your uncle, right? And Mary Partlain?"

"My father's cousin. And Brantley is my uncle Bevill's eldest son."

"And in what possible way is this a fair tribunal?"

"You'll have your say. It's more than you gave Clinton."

"Oh, he had his say." Anger eclipsed fear as the images from that terrible night flooded her brain, driving out everything but rage at what Clinton Bradbury had forced her to do to defend herself. "He said a lot of profane and wicked things to me before he tried to pin me to my bed, strip off my clothes and violate my body against my will."

"You're wasting your breath on me, Susan. I am not the one you'll need to convince." Even as he spoke, the van pulled to a stop.

Kenny Bradbury cut the engine and turned around to look at Asa. "We're here."

Asa rose to his feet and reached across to open the panel van's side door. Attached to him by the handcuff, Susannah had no choice but to rise as well, following him out of the van into the cold night air. Her ragged breath condensed as it hit the cold air, mingling with the misty swirls of Asa's slower, calmer exhalations.

In silence, he led her to an angled door, well-hidden by high-growing grass, about ten yards from the small, silent cabin that slumbered in the clearing. Surrounded by towering evergreens and autumn-hued hardwoods already starting to shed their leaves for the winter, the clearing was overgrown and littered with fallen leaves that crunched beneath Susannah's boots as she stumbled after him, tugged along by the handcuff and the sheer strength of Asa Bradbury's determination.

He waited for Kenny to unlock the padlock holding the cellar door closed, then nudged Susannah down a set of cinder-block stairs descending into the dark belly of the root cellar. With a tug of a chain, he turned on the only light in the room, a bald bulb screwed into a fixture attached to an exposed wooden beam in the cellar's unfinished ceiling.

He gave her a prod toward an old, battered sofa someone had pushed up against one of the cellar's dirt walls. "Sit."

She did as he ordered, gauging her chances at making a run for her life. Not good, she decided as he deftly removed the cuff around his wrist and slid it through one link of a chain hanging from a hook in the ceiling. "You should have enough chain to reach the toilet if you need it," he said, waving his hand toward a portable toilet chair standing nearby. "And you should be comfortable enough sleeping. I suggest you try to rest. There's not a lot of night left."

Without saying anything more to her, he headed back up the steps and disappeared through the door, closing it behind him. She heard the rattle of the padlock being reengaged.

Then there was nothing but silence, broken only by the thunderous cadence of her own pulse in her ears.

She checked her watch. Only four hours had passed since she and Hunter had left Quinn's cabin for their mission at the hotel.

Hunter, she thought, her heart sinking. What if she'd been wrong? What if he'd really been unconscious, or worse? She'd seen him breathing—she'd been able to reassure herself of that much, at least. But he might have sustained a closed head injury. His brain might be swelling right now, deadly pressure building in his skull.

Why hadn't she made them let her check on him?

How could she have left him behind that way?

She had to get out of here. Yes, the cellar door was padlocked, and yes, she was handcuffed to a chain, but there were ways of getting out of handcuffs, right? All she had to do was find the right tool.

The cellar was mostly bare—probably cleaned out specifically to make sure she wouldn't find anything to aid in her escape. But after a few minutes of searching, and stretching the chain to its limit, she found an old mesh bag of what looked to be desiccated, rotted potatoes. The blackened lumps only vaguely resembled their original state, and the smell rising from the bag was less than pleasant. But the bag itself was tied at one end by a metal twist tie. Susannah unwound the tie from the bag and stripped away the paper coating to reveal a thin, flexible wire.

"That'll do," she murmured with satisfaction, returning to the sofa and bending the wire in an L-shape. Before her grandmother had pulled her out of her father's home, she'd learned a few lessons in, well, less-than-legal arts. One of those things had been how to pick a handcuff lock.

The wire her father had used to teach her had been a twisted paper clip, which was considerably stiffer and less flexible than the twist tie she was currently applying to the handcuff lock. But with some finesse and, she had to admit, a whole lot of luck, she managed to get the wire in just the right position to spring the lock. The cuff fell open and she pulled her hand free, elated.

But her elation seeped away almost immediately. She'd won only the first battle, she knew, her gaze sliding toward the closed cellar doors at the top of the cinder-block stairs. The next part of the war would be the hardest. She had to figure out a way to get rid of the padlock trapping her in place.

From the inside, without a single tool at her disposal.

Chapter Sixteen

Hunter parked near the top of the ridge and consulted the map application on the burner phone Quinn had provided. Based on a few calculations and some extrapolation of information he'd found online, he figured that Laurel Bald should be dead ahead as the crow flew.

He lifted the binoculars he'd packed and peered through the predawn gloom. The night was mostly clear, but cold and damp enough for mists to settle into the coves and valleys between the rounded mountain peaks, partially obscuring his view.

After a few moments, however, his eyes adjusted to the darkness and a faint paleness began to separate itself from the gloom. A mostly treeless summit, dun-colored due to autumn dieoff—a bald, as it was known in this part of the Appalachians.

That had to be Laurel Bald, didn't it?

He scanned the mountain beneath the bald,

looking for signs of habitation. Most of the homes in Boneyard Ridge were scattered along the main road that wound its way around the mountain, denser in the lower elevations but growing more scattered where the road began to climb more steeply as it reached the summit.

There were a couple of houses located near the bald. He couldn't make out any lights from within the cabin walls, but slender fingers of smoke rose from stone chimneys to mingle with the mountain mists.

He punched in the number of Quinn's latest burner phone.

His boss answered on the first ring. "Still alive?"

"So far. Don't suppose you've had any luck analyzing those herbs?"

"This soon? No. I'm going to make some calls come daylight, though. See if we can't get the cop conference put on hold. I know some people high up in that law enforcement society—they'll listen to me."

"Why didn't you just do that in the first place?"

"I wanted to see what you could come up with first. It's a hell of a lot easier to go to them with all the information you and Ms. Marsh managed to put together than to go in there with nothing concrete to offer."

There was a lot Quinn wasn't saying, but

Hunter didn't have time to sort through his boss's half-truths and lies of omission. "Any chance you could give me some insight on the Bradburys before I go running in there half-cocked?"

"I was hoping you'd put the brakes on long enough to ask a pertinent question or two," Quinn said, grim amusement tinting his voice. "There are three main branches of the family, but only one you really need to worry about—Asa Bradbury, the younger of Aaron Bradbury's two sons and the head of the family now that the old man and Clinton are gone. Old Aaron had two brothers, Colton and Bevill, but Bevill had a stroke several years ago and he's disabled. His son Brantley has taken over for his father in the family business but he's not that interested in getting his hands dirty. And Colton's getting old now, so his son Kenny's doing a lot of the work of transporting drugs and keeping their dealers from getting any ideas about branching out on their own. He's more brawn than brains."

"Asa must have been the one doing all the talking tonight." Hunter pushed his hand through his short-cropped hair, wincing as his fingertips brushed over the painful lump at the back of his head. "He mentioned a tribunal tomorrow at ten. They're actually pretending to put her on trial?"

"Some of these old hill families see themselves

as the law in their own little enclaves. You ought to know that, growing up in Bitterwood."

"So we have until ten in the morning to get her out of there."

"You ready for that backup I offered?"

He thought about it. "I'd like them in position. I'm parked at an overlook right now that could work as a staging area. It's far enough from Laurel Bald that I think they'd be safe gathering here. I need to go in alone, see if I can get her out of there without raising a big ruckus, but it would be real nice to have backup close enough that they can help us get out of there if things go bad before we can get to safety."

"Give me the coordinates and I'll get everyone in position. You're going in now, I presume?"

"Yeah. I've spotted a turnoff about a quarter mile from the bald that should give me a place to leave the SUV and strike out on foot."

"You up to that? You took a hell of a knock to the head. I saw the lump. That wasn't a love tap."

"I'm fine," Hunter answered. It was mostly the truth. His head hurt, yes, but primarily on the outside. He wasn't dizzy or confused. The past few days of hiking had actually built up his stamina, rather than reduced it.

And even if none of that had been true, he would still be heading up the mountain after Susannah.

"Backup's on the way. You have Sutton Calhoun's cell number memorized?"

"I do."

"He'll be the point man, then. Call him and he'll take care of getting the backup crew where you need them." Quinn hung up without another word.

Pocketing the phone, Hunter started the SUV engine and pulled out of the overlook parking area and back onto the two-lane mountain road.

WHAT SHE NEEDED was an ax. She could chop through the weathered wood of the cellar door without worrying about the padlock if she just had an ax. Unfortunately, Asa Bradbury hadn't seen fit to leave such a tool at her disposal. Nor could she have tried unscrewing the hinges—not that she had a screwdriver—because the hinges were on the outside of the door.

No ax. No screwdriver. No hope.

She backed down the cinder-block stairs and settled on the musty old sofa, tears of despair pricking her eyes. She fought against them, both the tears and the despair, determined not to be paralyzed just because she hadn't yet found an easy solution.

A quick glance at her watch told her she still had several hours left before the tribunal. Part of her, the bleary-headed, gritty-eyed part, wanted to spend that time asleep. Surely the only thing worse than running out of time was spending what was left of her time on earth futilely beating her head against a cinder-block wall she had no hope of tearing down.

But what if Hunter needed her? What if he was still lying on the floor in the hotel basement, his brain swelling past the point of no return? What if she could save him if she could just find her way out of here and reach a phone?

A soft, swishing sound coming from outside the cellar door drew her attention back to her current problem. The sound grew closer, then stopped. For a long moment, there was no sound at all except for the thudding of her pulse in her ears.

Then she heard the faint rattle of metal against metal.

Someone had just moved the padlock.

Panic setting in, she reached for the handcuff dangling from the chain and slipped it around her wrist, stopping just short of clicking it shut. If her visitor outside was Asa or one of the other Bradburys, maybe they wouldn't look too closely at the cuff.

As she waited, breathless, the furtive metal-on-metal noises continued, barely there, and she realized whoever might be working on the padlock outside, it wasn't anyone who had a key.

Which meant it wasn't one of the Bradburys.

Slipping the cuff from her wrist, she quietly crossed to the stairs and climbed until she could put her eye against the narrow slit between the double cellar doors. She could see almost nothing through the narrow space, the darkness outside nearly complete.

But she could hear someone breathing, a soft whisper of respiration that seemed so familiar she almost thought she was imagining it.

Was she hearing what she wanted to hear? Panic could play terrible tricks with a person's mind, and she was about as scared as she'd ever been in her whole life.

But she had to take a chance. If she was imagining things, if there was nobody out there at all, what could it hurt?

"Help me," she said, her voice little more than a whisper.

For a second, the world around her went thick with silence again. Then she heard a whisper in return. "Susannah?"

Her knees wobbled, forcing her to grab the inside handle of the door to keep from tumbling backward down the cinder-block stairs. "Hunter?"

"It's me, baby. I found you. I just—I don't have anything to pick this lock. Your friends took my gun and my knife, and stupidly, I didn't pack another one."

"I did," she whispered back to him. "I found one at Quinn's place, and I didn't have room in my pack, so I stuck it in yours. But I forgot to get it before we hiked to the hotel. It's in one of the inner pockets."

She heard a rustling noise and then a soft murmur of excitement. "You wonderful, wonderful woman."

"Don't try picking the lock. Use the screwdriver blade and just unscrew the door hinges." Tamping down the flood of excitement that threatened to swamp her senses completely, she added, "But be careful. The Bradburys may be on the lookout for an escape attempt."

"I'm keeping an eye out. And I'm not alone. There are six other agents from The Gates out here in the woods behind me. I called in backup."

She heard a new rasping sound, coming from the right side of the door. He must be attacking the hinges now. She settled on the steps, listening to the sounds of his handiwork, and realized she'd been wrong about miracles.

Being snatched from the hotel parking lot and hauled off into the woods by this maddening, marvelous man had been one of the most miraculous things that had ever happened to her.

Considering how slowly time had been passing

since Asa Bradbury had dumped her in this cellar, it seemed only a few seconds later that Hunter whispered through the door, "Let's give it a go."

She turned to watch as Hunter eased the door away from the hinge. The padlock didn't allow the door to move much, but the narrow opening provided enough space for Susannah to slide through and scramble onto the grass outside.

Before she had a chance to say a word, Hunter had scooped her up and started running with her. A heartbeat later, the sharp bark of a pistol explained his sudden flight.

Someone was shooting at them.

ASA BRADBURY HAD been eighteen years old when his brother Clinton broke into Myra Stokes's neat little cabin with the intention of claiming Myra's granddaughter for himself. Asa had had one foot out of town, a hardship scholarship to Tennessee in his pocket and visions of a life outside the claustrophobic rock bluffs of Boneyard Ridge when his mother had walked into the bedroom he shared with his older brother and informed him that Clinton was dead.

"You're the head of the family now," she'd said, her voice like steel beneath her tears. "You know what you have to do."

Oh, he'd known. But he hadn't liked it.

Still didn't.

But that's what came from being trapped in a life he didn't want. His choices had been stripped away that cold November night. Just as he had no choice now but to go after the McKenzie girl and the man who'd stolen her away.

He didn't waste time wondering what would happen if he called off the pursuit. He might be the alpha dog in this pack, but there were hungry young curs circling his position, waiting for any sign of weakness.

There was no walking away from the life he'd inherited. No different path available to him, the way it had been available so briefly, a tantalizing prize just out of his reach, until Clinton's death.

Murder, he thought. He should call it murder. That's how the family still spoke of Clinton's death, as if it had been an act of evil perpetrated by a selfish, venal, young temptress.

But Asa drew the line at lying to himself. He knew what Clinton had been like. The impulse-control problems. The colossal sense of entitlement that had come with inheriting control of the Bradbury family business long before he was ready for it.

Asa hadn't been ready for it, either. But at least he'd been smart enough to do whatever it took to learn how to be a ruthless mountain drug lord before the circling wolves could take him out.

One of those lessons was about the folly of mercy. Mercy was a sign of weakness. There was no place for mercy in the world in which Asa and his family lived. So the girl had to face the tribunal. And her protector had to be eliminated.

That was the law of the hills. The law of the Bradburys.

Swallowing a sigh of frustration, Asa reloaded his Winchester .700 and followed his kinsmen into the woods.

A BULLET WHIPPED past Hunter's ear and hit the tree beside him, sending wood and bark shrapnel flying. A splinter grazed his forehead but he kept running, pushing Susannah ahead of him as they scrambled through the underbrush, heading deeper into the forest.

The straighter path to the place where he'd left the SUV would have been to head right over the bald, but the dearth of trees would have made them easy targets for whoever was behind them taking potshots. They were lucky to have gotten a head start; if the person snapping off rounds at them were better with that rifle he was wielding, they might both be dead already.

"Left!" Susannah threw the word over her shoulder, letting the cold morning breeze carry the word back to Hunter as she jogged left, into a dense thicket of mountain laurel bushes. He had to fight his way through, with no time for stealth or hiding their trail. He wasn't sure there was any way to sneak out of these woods without the Bradburys following them.

But apparently Susannah had a different idea. Almost as soon as they'd reached the middle of the mountain laurel thicket, she stopped, tugging him to the ground with her. They crouched there, trying to slow their breathing and listen for any sign of their pursuers.

After a long spell of silence, Susannah reached for his hand, closing her fingers tightly around his. In the pale light of predawn, her eyes reflected the first faint rose hues of sunrise, dark with emotion. "I was so scared," she whispered.

He cupped her cheek with one hand. "I know. I'm sorry I let them take you, but—"

"But you came after me." She slid her hand over his, holding it in place. "I thought I saw your eyelids move, when you were lying there, but I wasn't sure. I started to second-guess myself. I was so afraid you were really hurt, and I'd left you there to die—"

He touched his forehead to hers. "I've got a hard head."

She fell silent for a few moments, just letting him hold her. Finally, however, she pulled her head away from his, drawing a deep breath.

"They're out there. I can't hear them, but I can feel them."

"I know." He felt them, too, like a gathering storm.

"You said you have backup?"

"They're on the way. I called them in as soon as I spotted the cabins."

"How did you know where to look for me?"

"Honestly? I didn't." He'd never felt more helpless in his life than he'd felt as he crouched there on the edge of the clearing, wondering how on earth he was supposed to find Susannah and get her away from the Bradburys without getting both of them killed. "I was sneaking around the cabin, trying to see if I could find any sign that you were even there, when I almost stumbled over the root cellar doors hidden in the high grass. The door itself was faded and weathered, but the padlock holding it shut looked shiny and new. Got me to wondering."

She flashed him a quick smile. "Smart man."

God, he wanted to kiss her. It was the worst possible time for sentimentality, but he was so damn glad to see her still alive and well.

"I think we're going to have to make a run for it. Before they have time to surround us," he said.

"What if we're already too late?"

He brushed her jaw with his fingertips. "It's a chance we have to take. Ready?"

She stared at him, her eyes wide and scared. But her jaw jutted forward, her expression made of solid mountain granite. She gave a short nod. "Ready."

He pushed to his feet, tugging her up with him.

And six rifles cocked in a stutter of metallic clicks, their long barrels surrounding Hunter and Susannah on all sides.

Chapter Seventeen

"Take her back to the cabin." Asa Bradbury spoke in a low, bored tone that sent a hard, racking chill down Susannah's spine. "I'll take care of her friend."

"No!" She took a rushing step toward Asa, but Hunter's hand closed around her arm, pulling her back.

"Go with them," he said quietly.

"No!" She wrapped her arms around him tightly, trying to surround him completely with her body. "If they're going to kill us both, then they can damn well kill us together."

"Very touching," Asa drawled, as tonelessly as if he were remarking on the weather on a mild day.

She shot a look at him over her shoulder, hating him in a way she never had before. She'd been running and hiding from Asa and his kin for years, but she'd never hated him the way she'd hated Clinton. She'd always seen Asa as collateral damage, the Bradbury who'd gotten sucked into this blood vendetta against his will.

But looking at him now, seeing how little he cared about her life, one way or another, she finally understood what the philosopher Hannah Arendt had meant when she wrote of the banality of evil. Under any other circumstances, Asa Bradbury might have been an ordinary man, living an ordinary life, not hurting anyone and maybe contributing something meaningful to the world.

But he'd taken the path of least resistance and let his family's corruption swallow him whole. He wasn't driven by greed or hate or any emotion that might make sense of his determination to see her dead.

He was driven by inertia. And that's what made him truly frightening.

Hunter's arms tightened around her suddenly, pulling her closer. He pressed his lips to her temple and let them slide lightly down her cheek to her ear. "Duck," he whispered, and pushed her down to the ground.

"Drop your weapons!" The voice, hard and commanding, boomed through the woods around them, amplified by a bullhorn.

Hunter rolled over on top of her, pressing her to the ground beneath his body as chaos erupted around them. She heard a cacophony of shouts and curses, punctuated by a couple of gunshots, close by. Hunter tucked her even more firmly beneath him, whispering reassurances in her ear that she felt more than heard.

Over the bullhorn, the deep voice rang again. "You're surrounded. Put down your weapons and no one has to die today."

The chaos subsided into a strange, uneasy silence. Then she heard the sound of grass swishing, bushes rustling, and within her limited range of vision, she saw Kenny Bradbury bend and drop his Winchester to the ground.

A minute later, the voice she'd heard over the bullhorn spoke again, without amplification and so close her nerves jerked. "Situation contained, Bragg. You injured?"

Hunter rolled away from her and pushed to his knees. He helped her into a kneeling position as well, not answering his colleague as he looked her over with an anxious gaze. "You okay? Anything hurt?"

She shook her head, finding speech beyond her capacity at the moment.

The man who'd spoken earlier crouched beside her, flashing her a brief smile that displayed a set of dimples nearly as disarming as Hunter's. "We're going to have a talk with these folks, okay?" He waved one of the other agents from The Gates over, a slim brunette woman dressed in the same woodland camouflage pattern worn by the rest of the agents who were gathering discarded rifles and herding the Bradburys toward their cabins.

"I'm Ava," the brunette introduced herself. She glanced warily at Hunter, as if she expected him to protest. When he remained silent, she ventured a smile at Susannah. "Let's get you out of here."

Hunter might not have resisted, but Susannah did. "Hunter—"

"Ava will take care of you. I need to stay here, just for a bit."

She lowered her voice. "What are y'all going to do?"

A feral light gleamed in Hunter's green eyes. "We're going to let the Bradburys know just how things are going to go from now on."

"It's my fight. Don't trundle me off like I'm the girl."

"You *are* the girl." He touched her face, his lips curving. "My girl."

"Don't make me go all Gloria Steinem on you—"

"If she wants in on this, let her in." The man still holding the bullhorn shrugged. "She's right. It's her fight, too."

Hunter shot the other man a frown that might have alarmed a weaker man, but the man with the bullhorn didn't even react.

Signaling his surrender with a deep sigh, Hunter threaded his fingers through hers and nodded toward the line of agents still pushing the Bradburys through the woods ahead of them. "Come on, let's get this over with. I'd like to get back to the hotel in time to watch your buddy Marcus get what's coming to him."

"THIS IS HOW it's going to go." Hunter stood in front of the group of disarmed Bradbury kinsmen, scanning the room carefully for any sign of impending insurrection before he settled his gaze on the Bradbury in charge.

Asa Bradbury looked for all the world like a slightly shabby accountant, all lean angles and a nebbish sort of averageness. His brown eyes were sharp but mostly devoid of emotion as he held Hunter's gaze without speaking. There wasn't even a hint of the sullen anger he saw in the faces of Bradbury's kinsmen, only a tepid sort of resignation.

"Susan McKenzie is dead. She no longer exists. Your blood vendetta is over as of now." Hunter paced slowly in front of the subdued group of Bradburys who now sat facing him, but his gaze never left Asa's face. "Any attempt to cause any problem whatsoever for the woman named Susannah Marsh will be met with any and all force necessary to make you and yours wish you'd never been born. She's under the protection of The Gates now. You do not want to test our resolve."

Asa Bradbury's gaze didn't waver. He said just one word. "Understood."

Hunter finally released his gaze and looked at Susannah, who stood next to Ava Trent a couple of feet away. Susannah's winter-sky eyes glittered with an emotion that did more to make his knees quiver than anything that had happened to this point.

His fellow agent Sutton Calhoun stepped forward, still holding the bullhorn dangling from one hand. "Your weapons have been emptied of ammunition and left in the root cellar where you were keeping Susannah Marsh. Please don't do anything foolish that might necessitate our returning here in the future." He nodded toward Hunter.

Hunter crossed to Susannah and took her hand. "Let's go."

Flanked by Sutton and Ava, they left the Bradbury cabin and started the long walk back to the staging area.

SUSANNAH HAD NEVER felt more tired in her life than she felt at the moment, slumped in the executive chair in front of her desk in the office she'd called her home away from home for the past two years. The small clock on her desk blotter read 7:00 a.m.

Marcus Lemonde should be walking through the door any minute.

"You don't have to be here. I'm not really sure you should." Perched on the edge of her desk, Hunter slanted a worried look in her direction.

"Wouldn't miss it for the world," she assured him.

Alexander Quinn was seated at Marcus's desk, his posture relaxed. He was conversing quietly with the fourth person occupying the office, Ridge County Sheriff's Department lieutenant Hale Borden, a tall, lean man in his early forties, with thinning flax-colored hair and sharp blue eyes. He was in civilian clothes, but there was no missing the bulge of his service pistol tucked in a holster at his hip, ill-concealed beneath his suit jacket.

Quinn had called in a favor from the Ridge County sheriff himself, using the county's crime lab to rush the testing of the spice jars Hunter had handed over. "There were several ounces of belladonna leaves in the basil and the oregano that was slotted for the wine reduction the caterer was going to use for both the chicken and mushroom dishes," Quinn had told them as soon as they drove up to the hotel. "Enough to make everyone extremely sick—or worse. They executed a search of his desk a few minutes ago and found what looks like more belladonna leaves. I think we've got him."

There were four deputies, also dressed as civilians, waiting for Marcus Lemonde's arrival. They would follow him to the office to make sure he didn't give Lt. Borden any trouble.

Across the office, Borden's cell phone hummed. He checked the display screen and nodded at Quinn. "Showtime."

A couple of minutes later, the office door opened and Marcus Lemonde entered, his gaze lowered, focusing on the cell phone in his hand.

The look of dismayed shock on his face as he took in his four unexpected visitors was everything Susannah had hoped for.

"Marcus Lemonde, you're under arrest for conspiracy to commit murder," Lt. Borden informed him cheerfully.

Marcus turned to run but the four trailing deputies blocked his exit, pushing him back into the office.

Wild-eyed, Marcus looked back at Susannah, then noticed Hunter sitting on the edge of her desk. His eyes widened with surprise.

"Hi again," Hunter said with a satisfied smile. "Remember me?"

"ARE THE CHARGES going to stick?" Susannah's voice was thick with weariness.

She'd been silent for most of the drive to Quinn's cabin, so her sleepy question came as a jolt to Hunter's nervous system. He glanced at her, taking in her heavy-lidded gaze. "Quinn thinks so. The lab didn't get any prints off the bottles, but the search of Marcus's desk yielded more belladonna leaves. Since the police didn't use our testimony of finding the leaves in the drawer to get the warrant to search the desk, it should stand up to legal scrutiny."

"Do you think the BRI will target you for your part in the sting?"

"Spoken like a woman who's spent the past twelve years running from a blood vendetta."

Her lips curved slightly. "Well, if you need me to go all commando on the BRI for you, you know where to find me."

"Will I?" he asked, almost afraid to hear her answer.

She turned her gaze toward him slowly. "You think I'm planning to go to ground again? Change my name, cut my hair, find a new place to live?"

"Wouldn't be the first time."

"No, it wouldn't." She leaned her head back against the seat. "But I like it here in Ridge County. I missed the hills when I was gone, and

I'm getting too old and too settled in my ways to keep running."

"Are you worried about the Bradburys?"

She shook her head. "Asa's heart was never really in it, you know. And I think you and your pals at The Gates made your point."

Quinn's cabin came into view, and Hunter fell silent the rest of the way, pondering how to bring up the next question he wanted to ask. Getting her to agree to stick around Ridge County had been easier than he'd anticipated, given her past. He wouldn't have blamed her if she'd wanted a fresh start.

Hell, he might have offered to go with her.

She staggered a little as she started up the porch steps. Hunter caught her before she fell, closing his hands over her elbows as he walked her to the door. He still had Quinn's key in his pocket—the Bradburys hadn't bothered to take it from him when they patted him down. He unlocked the door and nudged her inside ahead of him.

She made it as far as the sofa before she slumped onto the plush cushions and gazed up at him, bleary-eyed. "I could sleep for a week."

He settled next to her, nudging her shoulder with his own. "Before you drift off, Sleeping Beauty, there's something I need to ask you."

Rolling her head onto his shoulder, she looked up at him. "I hope it's not an overly complex question."

"It might be," he admitted, nuzzling his nose against her forehead. "It's about the future. Specifically, your future. And mine."

She sat up and looked at him, her eyes sharpening. "Is this a question or a proposition?"

He couldn't quell a grin. "Possibly both."

Her lips curved slowly in response. "Well, the proposition part might need to be tabled until I get some sleep."

"I think we have something between us. Something good." He grimaced, feeling inarticulate. "I think maybe I'm in love with you."

The curve of her lips deepened, and her soft gray eyes flashed a hint of fire. "Maybe?"

"Probably."

"That's marginally better."

"Most likely?"

She bent toward him, brushing her smiling lips against his. "Getting warmer."

Definitely, he thought as her kiss sparked a thousand little fires along his nervous system.

Her fingers playing at the back of his neck, she tugged him closer, her lips parting to deepen the kiss. Her tongue tangled with his before she slowly pulled away to gaze up at him with desire-drunk eyes.

"Lucky for you, I'm most likely falling in love with you, too." She plucked lightly at the top button of his shirt, stopping tantalizingly short of pulling it out of the buttonhole. "And I will definitely prove it to you soon."

"After you sleep for a week?" he murmured against her temple.

"See?" She smoothed her fingers over his chest, making his heart pound. "It's like we can read each other's minds."

She settled in the curve of his arm, warm and sleepy and perfect. After a few minutes, her breathing slowed and deepened as she drifted to sleep.

Relaxing deeper into the sofa cushions, Hunter let himself watch her for a few moments before he eased from beneath her and stretched her out on the sofa, covering her with the fuzzy brown blanket draped over the arm. She made a soft grumbling noise but curled up under the blanket and went back to sleep.

Hunter walked quietly into the kitchen and pulled out the burner phone Quinn had given him back at the hotel before he and Susannah had left for the cabin. "I think there's a call you need to make. Don't you?" Quinn had asked.

Settling in one of the kitchen chairs, Hunter

punched in the number and made himself push SEND. A couple of rings later, he heard the familiar timbre of his sister Janet's voice. "Hello?"

"Hey, Jannie," he said. "It's me."

"My God, Hunter! I've been so worried about you! Are you okay?"

Tears pricking his eyes, he smiled at the warm autumn sunlight drifting through the kitchen windows. "I'm fine," he answered. "Just fine."

"Where are you? What have you been doing?"

He couldn't hold back a watery laugh. "That's a long, interesting story, Jannie. You got a minute to hear it?"

"Are you kidding? Of course I do."

In her voice, he heard a hint of worry and a lot of curiosity, but not a single ounce of censure, even though he had been out of touch for far too long and, as far as she knew, doing something she hated. Her love for him was unconditional, and most of the time he felt entirely unworthy of it.

As he thumbed away the tears that escaped his eyes, he heard soft footsteps behind him. Turning, he saw Susannah standing in the kitchen doorway, looking sleep-tousled and irresistible. Her shapely eyebrows lifted in a question, and he stretched his hand toward her.

She crossed to the table and put her hand in his, letting him tug her down to his lap. Curling her arms around his shoulders, she nestled into his embrace, her head tucked in the curve of his neck.

"Hunter?" Janet's voice buzzed in his ear.

Leaning his head against Susannah's, he let go of his tension in a soft sigh. "Ever heard of a private investigation firm called The Gates?"

* * * * *

Look for more books in award-winning author Paula Graves's miniseries THE GATES in 2015. You'll find them wherever Harlequin Intrigue books are sold.

LARGER-PRINT BOOKS!

HARLEQUIN *Presents*

PASSION GUARANTEED SEDUCTION

GET 2 FREE LARGER-PRINT NOVELS PLUS 2 FREE GIFTS!

YES! Please send me 2 FREE LARGER-PRINT Harlequin Presents® novels and my 2 FREE gifts (gifts are worth about $10). After receiving them, if I don't wish to receive any more books, I can return the shipping statement marked "cancel." If I don't cancel, I will receive 6 brand-new novels every month and be billed just $5.05 per book in the U.S. or $5.49 per book in Canada. That's a saving of at least 16% off the cover price! It's quite a bargain! Shipping and handling is just 50¢ per book in the U.S. and 75¢ per book in Canada.* I understand that accepting the 2 free books and gifts places me under no obligation to buy anything. I can always return a shipment and cancel at any time. Even if I never buy another book, the two free books and gifts are mine to keep forever.

176/376 HDN F43N

Name	(PLEASE PRINT)	
Address		Apt. #
City	State/Prov.	Zip/Postal Code

Signature (if under 18, a parent or guardian must sign)

Mail to the **Harlequin® Reader Service:**
IN U.S.A.: P.O. Box 1867, Buffalo, NY 14240-1867
IN CANADA: P.O. Box 609, Fort Erie, Ontario L2A 5X3

**Are you a subscriber to Harlequin Presents books
and want to receive the larger-print edition?
Call 1-800-873-8635 today or visit us at www.ReaderService.com.**

* Terms and prices subject to change without notice. Prices do not include applicable taxes. Sales tax applicable in N.Y. Canadian residents will be charged applicable taxes. Offer not valid in Quebec. This offer is limited to one order per household. Not valid for current subscribers to Harlequin Presents Larger-Print books. All orders subject to credit approval. Credit or debit balances in a customer's account(s) may be offset by any other outstanding balance owed by or to the customer. Please allow 4 to 6 weeks for delivery. Offer available while quantities last.

Your Privacy—The Harlequin® Reader Service is committed to protecting your privacy. Our Privacy Policy is available online at www.ReaderService.com or upon request from the Harlequin Reader Service.

We make a portion of our mailing list available to reputable third parties that offer products we believe may interest you. If you prefer that we not exchange your name with third parties, or if you wish to clarify or modify your communication preferences, please visit us at www.ReaderService.com/consumerchoice or write to us at Harlequin Reader Service Preference Service, P.O. Box 9062, Buffalo, NY 14269. Include your complete name and address.

HPLP13R

LARGER-PRINT BOOKS!

GET 2 FREE LARGER-PRINT NOVELS PLUS
2 FREE GIFTS!

✦ HARLEQUIN®

Romance

From the Heart, For the Heart

YES! Please send me 2 FREE LARGER-PRINT Harlequin® Romance novels and my 2 FREE gifts (gifts are worth about $10). After receiving them, if I don't wish to receive any more books, I can return the shipping statement marked "cancel." If I don't cancel, I will receive 4 brand-new novels every month and be billed just $4.84 per book in the U.S. or $5.24 per book in Canada. That's a savings of at least 19% off the cover price! It's quite a bargain! Shipping and handling is just 50¢ per book in the U.S. and 75¢ per book in Canada.* I understand that accepting the 2 free books and gifts places me under no obligation to buy anything. I can always return a shipment and cancel at any time. Even if I never buy another book, the two free books and gifts are mine to keep forever.

119/319 HDN F43Y

Name	(PLEASE PRINT)

Address		Apt. #

City	State/Prov.	Zip/Postal Code

Signature (if under 18, a parent or guardian must sign)

Mail to the Harlequin® Reader Service:
IN U.S.A.: P.O. Box 1867, Buffalo, NY 14240-1867
IN CANADA: P.O. Box 609, Fort Erie, Ontario L2A 5X3

Want to try two free books from another line?
Call 1-800-873-8635 or visit www.ReaderService.com.

* Terms and prices subject to change without notice. Prices do not include applicable taxes. Sales tax applicable in N.Y. Canadian residents will be charged applicable taxes. Offer not valid in Quebec. This offer is limited to one order per household. Not valid for current subscribers to Harlequin Romance Larger-Print books. All orders subject to credit approval. Credit or debit balances in a customer's account(s) may be offset by any other outstanding balance owed by or to the customer. Please allow 4 to 6 weeks for delivery. Offer available while quantities last.

Your Privacy—The Harlequin® Reader Service is committed to protecting your privacy. Our Privacy Policy is available online at www.ReaderService.com or upon request from the Harlequin Reader Service.

We make a portion of our mailing list available to reputable third parties that offer products we believe may interest you. If you prefer that we not exchange your name with third parties, or if you wish to clarify or modify your communication preferences, please visit us at www.ReaderService.com/consumerschoice or write to us at Harlequin Reader Service Preference Service, P.O. Box 9062, Buffalo, NY 14269. Include your complete name and address.

HRLP13R

LARGER-PRINT BOOKS!
GET 2 FREE LARGER-PRINT NOVELS PLUS
2 FREE GIFTS!

HARLEQUIN®

super romance®

More Story...More Romance

YES! Please send me 2 FREE LARGER-PRINT Harlequin® Superromance® novels and my 2 FREE gifts (gifts are worth about $10). After receiving them, if I don't wish to receive any more books, I can return the shipping statement marked "cancel." If I don't cancel, I will receive 6 brand-new novels every month and be billed just $5.69 per book in the U.S. or $5.99 per book in Canada. That's a savings of at least 16% off the cover price! It's quite a bargain! Shipping and handling is just 50¢ per book in the U.S. or 75¢ per book in Canada.* I understand that accepting the 2 free books and gifts places me under no obligation to buy anything. I can always return a shipment and cancel at any time. Even if I never buy another book, the two free books and gifts are mine to keep forever.

139/339 HDN F46Y

Name	(PLEASE PRINT)	

Address		Apt. #

City	State/Prov.	Zip/Postal Code

Signature (if under 18, a parent or guardian must sign)

Mail to the **Harlequin**® **Reader Service:**
IN U.S.A.: P.O. Box 1867, Buffalo, NY 14240-1867
IN CANADA: P.O. Box 609, Fort Erie, Ontario L2A 5X3

Are you a current subscriber to Harlequin Superromance books and want to receive the larger-print edition?
Call 1-800-873-8635 today or visit www.ReaderService.com.

* Terms and prices subject to change without notice. Prices do not include applicable taxes. Sales tax applicable in N.Y. Canadian residents will be charged applicable taxes. Offer not valid in Quebec. This offer is limited to one order per household. Not valid for current subscribers to Harlequin Superromance Larger-Print books. All orders subject to credit approval. Credit or debit balances in a customer's account(s) may be offset by any other outstanding balance owed by or to the customer. Please allow 4 to 6 weeks for delivery. Offer available while quantities last.

Your Privacy—The Harlequin® Reader Service is committed to protecting your privacy. Our Privacy Policy is available online at www.ReaderService.com or upon request from the Harlequin Reader Service.

We make a portion of our mailing list available to reputable third parties that offer products we believe may interest you. If you prefer that we not exchange your name with third parties, or if you wish to clarify or modify your communication preferences, please visit us at www.ReaderService.com/consumerschoice or write to us at Harlequin Reader Service Preference Service, P.O. Box 9062, Buffalo, NY 14269. Include your complete name and address.

HSRLP13R